the Faber GUIDE

to twentieth-century ARCHITECTURE

BRITAIN and NORTHERN EUROPE

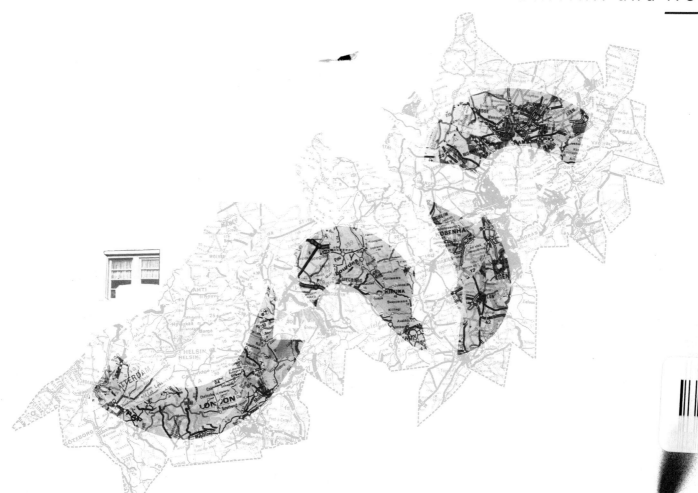

by Lance Knobel

First published in 1985
by Faber and Faber Limited
3 Queen Square London WC1

Design by Studio Dumbar, Holland
Jos Stoopman, Ruhi Hamid, Ton van Bragt
Artwork I. Chilvers
Filmset by
ADO Typesetting Limited, London WC1
Printed in Great Britain by
Jolly & Barber Ltd., Rugby, Warwickshire

British Library Cataloguing in Publication Data

Knobel, Lance
The Faber guide to twentieth-century
architecture: Britain and Northern Europe.
1. Architecture — — Europe 2. Architecture,
Modern — — 20th century — — Europe
I. Title
720'.94   NA958
ISBN 0-571-13556-0

Library of Congress Cataloguing in Publication Data

Knobel, Lance.
The Faber guide to twentieth-century architecture.
1. Architecture, Modern — — 20th century — — Guide-books.
I. Title. II. Title: Guide to twentieth-century
architecture. III. Title: Faber guide to 20th century
architecture.
NA680.K59 1985 724.9'1 84-25875
ISBN 0-571-13556-0

Contents

To my parents

Introduction

The idea for this book came from a personal need. Having studied and become fascinated by twentieth-century architecture, I naturally wanted to see the buildings that intrigued me in photographs. But unlike the architecture of earlier centuries, the buildings of our own century can rarely be found in guidebooks. In Europe, they usually hide in rarely visited residential or industrial districts remote from more familiar city centres, for in every generation architectural pioneers are forced to build away from the public gaze and the institutional pressures of conformity. Even in the histories of twentieth-century architecture, exact addresses of buildings are extremely rare. So in seeking out the great buildings of the twentieth-century, I was forced to dig in specialised libraries, to rely on other pilgrims and on locally knowledgeable architects and historians. Visiting the architecture of our century should not be so difficult, however, for there are many buildings that have profoundly affected the way we live and look at the world and that are works of art which can compare with the best of previous centuries.

There are also incidental rewards when seeing modern buildings. As many of them are off the beaten tourist track, visitors have a chance to discover unknown, unspoilt areas of the major cities of Europe. So, too, does one frequently discover other buildings lurking around a corner: art nouveau and Jugendstil architecture in particular seems to leave its imprint on whole neighbourhoods rather than on isolated buildings. But while I obviously encourage readers to keep their eyes open for twentieth-century works in addition to the 300 or so buildings in this guide, it is a mistake to be so blinkered that you neglect earlier architecture. For although much of the great architecture of our century marked a radical change from the styles of the past, no building derived from a complete break with tradition.

The buildings in this guide, necessarily a highly selective list, have been chosen for a number of reasons. I made an early decision to show only buildings that are publicly accessible: if a building hides behind a high wall that only mountaineers could scale it is not included. Buildings that are open to the public are indicated in the index by a ○. In the case of private buildings, however, please respect the privacy of the inhabitants. Usually a visit to see the interior of a private building can be arranged by writing in advance; most owners of great works are proud of their possession and feel a duty to allow visitors access. Further, no purely engineering works are included in the guide. Given these two basic criteria, reasons for choosing one building rather than another vary widely. Some are selected because of their influence on other architects, or because of their importance in the development of an individual architect's style. Other buildings have been selected because they are specially interesting examples of specific movements, styles or trends. Still others, admittedly, have been included for purely personal, idiosyncratic reasons of taste. The buildings are arranged by country and within countries by town. Within each town, works are ordered by the date the design was begun, to facilitate stylistic comparisons and trace influences. Cross-references to other works by individual architects can be found by consulting the index at the back.

Clearly in a book of this nature, there are numerous people who have offered advice and assistance, not least the many residents and owners of the buildings shown. But I should particularly like to thank David Coffin, Robert Clark and Ned Harwood of Princeton University who first fired my enthusiasm for architectural history; my colleagues at The Architectural Press who tolerated my hoarding of library books; Phil Sayer and the Derek Robinson Partnership for transforming my photographs into wonderful prints; Giles de la Mare and many of his colleagues for honing the manuscript into a book; Studio Dumbar for their design of the book; Gill Coleridge who made certain the book became more than an idea; and Anne Inglis who made certain it got done.

□

Photographic Acknowledgements

All photographs are by the author except:
◇ 13, Archives d'Architecture Moderne
◇ 16, Jørn Utzon
◇ 17-20, Jørgen Watz
◇ 21, K. Petersen
◇ 33, 38, 39, 42, 44, 45, Museum of Finnish Architecture
◇ 55, Editions du Cerf
◇ 56, 99, 100, 181, 183, 187, 190, 191, 200, 202, 205, 209, 224, 225, 227, 228, 230, 231, 232, 235, 236, 240, 241, 242, 245, 249, 251, 294, The Architectural Press
◇ 59, 72, 108, Architecture d'Aujourd'hui
◇ 61, Cement and Concrete Association
◇ 63, G. E. Kidder Smith
◇ 101, Masson Rayner
◇ 103, Ken Kirkwood
◇ 112, Patrick Hannay
◇ 130, Stadt Hagen
◇ 137, Landesamt für Denkmalpflege Schleswig-Holstein
◇ 140, Wim Cox
◇ 144, Beton-Verlag
◇ 156, Fotoarchiv Böttcherstrasse
◇ 185, 197, 250, Eric de Maré
◇ 188, Henk Snoek
◇ 196, Keith Gibson
◇ 199, André Goulancourt
◇ 201, 204, 254, Country Life
◇ 203, 246, John Donat
◇ 238, Richard Bryant
◇ 243, Richard Rogers and Partners
◇ 247, Martin Charles
◇ 256, John Trelawny-Ross
◇ 267, Rijksdienst v/d Monumentenzorg
◇ 272, KLM Aerocarto
◇ 274, P. A. C. Rook
◇ 279, Otto Vaering
◇ 280, Teignens Fotoatelier

◇ photograph numbers

the Faber GUIDE
to twentieth-century ARCHITECTURE

Belgium

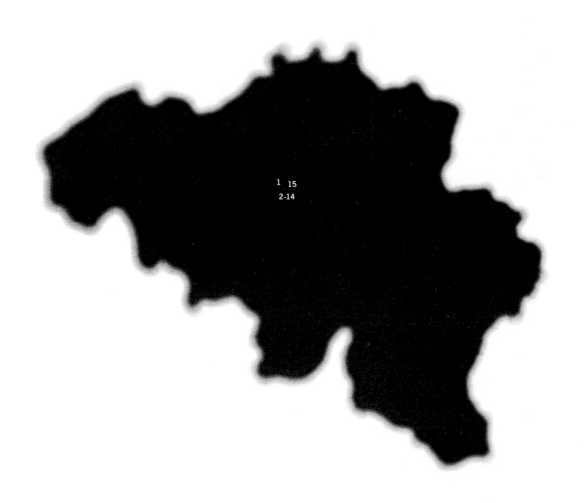

1 15
2-14

Bourgeois' Cité Moderne is the first example in the years after World War I of a large-scale development combining simple, modern architectural forms with loose, garden city planning. In this sense, it prefigures many better-known developments in Germany and elsewhere. Bourgeois realised the 300 housing units of the Cité Moderne at the age of twenty-five, after training at the Académie Royale des Beaux-Arts in Brussels and an apprenticeship with the National Society for Low-Cost Housing. The central square is perhaps the most interesting area: the zig-zag lines of the two blocks of housing flanking the square lead to the larger three-storey central block, housing shops and other public facilities. What once, in a model community, would have been the site for a church has now become the site of populist communal facilities. The larger houses suggest the influence of Frank Lloyd Wright on Bourgeois, with their overhanging eaves and strictly rectilinear composition. The flat roofs could even be a misinterpretation of Wright's prairie style houses, because the illustrations in the Wasmuth portfolio of Wright's work, widely circulated in Europe when Bourgeois was a student, used a perspective that hid the steeply pitched roofs that Wright actually used. Following the success of the Cité Moderne, Bourgeois became the leading Belgian representative in the international architectural world: he built a house in the 1927 Weissenhof-Siedlung and was at the first Congrès Internationaux d'Architecture Moderne (CIAM) at La Serraz in 1928.

□

Solvay house 1895-1900

2	224 avenue Louise Brussels	architect Victor Horta

The Solvay house was Horta's first great work, and, because of the destruction of so many of his buildings (most notably the Maison du Peuple), stands today as his finest extant building. Built on the then-new boulevard, the avenue Louise, for a wealthy family, the Solvay house has a tripartite façade: two tall bays project to frame a recessed centre. The bays are themselves divided into three by metal colonnettes and transoms. Within this overall symmetry, Horta's most inventive decorative ironwork flows around balconies and windows. The entrance itself, originally for carriages, is also symmetrical with the flowing woodwork bolstered at the bottom by a practical reinforcement of decorative ironwork.

Inside the entrance, paired iron piers stand in the hall (once the carriage drive). A wide flight of top-lit stairs leads to a landing adorned with a mural by Theo van Rysselberghe, who was Belgium's leading pointillist painter. On either side of the landing, the stairs continue to the piano nobile first floor. Throughout the house, Horta designed all the furniture and fittings as well as the extensive decorations. In the dining-room, for example, on the first floor overlooking the garden, a floral chandelier by Horta blooms above guests' heads. In the living-rooms overlooking the avenue, the music-room once contained a grand piano designed by Horta; a more philistine partner to this was the Horta-designed billiard table in the adjoining gentlemen's salon.

☐

Own house (now Horta museum) 1898-1911

3	23-25 rue Américaine Brussels	architect Victor Horta

Horta's own house and studio fall midway between the exuberance of the Solvay house ◇ 2 and the restraint of the Hallet house ◇ 10 . The stone front is flat, with almost no carving, for the ironwork carries the decorative burden. Above the entrance to the house, a square bay projects, with a balcony on the first floor. Here the intertwining of the decorative ironwork and the stone brackets are among Horta's finest exterior details. The ironwork also serves as support for the glazed canopy above the door. The studio next door stands in clear contrast to the house: its more sober image perhaps reflecting the professional work that went on inside. The continuous ribbon window set behind iron mullions is a foretaste of Horta's less distinctive architecture of his later years, but here it remains as an interesting foil to the more conventional art nouveau fenestration of the rest of the elevation. The interior, which Horta remodelled in 1911, is not among his best works.

☐

House 1900

| 4 | 41 place L. Morichard
Saint-Gilles, Brussels | architect
Ernest Blérot |

Blérot was among the more prolific art nouveau architects in Belgium, and his house on place Morichard is one of the better examples of his work. The three-storey house is basically conventional, but Blérot distorts the lines of the house with his inventive carved stone support for the first-storey oriel window. As with so many of the Brussels art nouveau houses, the windows and the associated ironwork have received most of the attention from the architect. Of particular interest here is the ironwork on the basement windows, and the iron balconies that seem to grow out of the oriel window.

□

Saint-Cyr house 1900

| 5 | 11 square Ambiorix
Brussels | architect
Gustave Strauven |

The thin four-storey house of Monsieur de Saint-Cyr is one of the most extreme surviving examples of the art nouveau. While Horta, at the same time, was carefully integrating his decoration and structure, intertwining ironwork and stone, Strauven seems to have been content to let his decorative fantasies run riot, particularly in the jungle of ironwork. Strauven actually worked as a draughtsman for Horta from 1896 to 1898, but he must have felt cramped by Horta's restraint if one can judge from the Saint-Cyr house. Strauven also was not hampered by Horta's relatively sparing use of materials: in the Saint-Cyr house stone, brick, glass, wood and ironwork all jostle for attention. Although this extreme exuberance is at first astounding, the lack of any restraint or calculation in the composition of the decoration is ultimately rather tiring.

□

Café Falstaff 1903

		architect
6	17-19 rue Henri Maus Brussels	E. Houbion

The Café Falstaff is among the few extant commercial works of the art nouveau. Most of the restaurants, cafés and shops executed in the style have drastically altered, if not completely destroyed both their façade and interior. But Falstaff, with its enormous eye-like round windows and sinuously curved mirrors, has been well preserved. The lettering of the sign between the two entrances seems more art deco than art nouveau, but it is original.

☐

Artist's residence and studio 1903

		architect
7	150-152 rue Potagère Schaerbeek, Brussels	Unknown

The artist's house and studio is one of the strangest of Brussels' many art nouveau works in the way it combines fairly sober decoration with the most fantastic of shapes. Where art nouveau usually means merely applied decoration, in the form of ironwork or carved stone, on rue Potagère the very shape of the building creates the characteristically restless impression of the art nouveau. The treatment of the ground and first floors is straightforward, with bud-like windows thrusting upwards. But the bay windows of the second floor, sprung out from the building like a sliding drawer, loom over the street. The 'rose' window above further unbalances the composition. Sadly, the painted floral decoration above the 'rose' window has now faded almost beyond recognition.

☐

Own house and studio 1905

8 | 5 rue des Francs
Etterbeek, Brussels

architect
Paul Cauchie

The connection between the Viennese Secessionists and art nouveau can clearly be seen in Cauchie's own house and studio, where his sgraffito panels recall the richer figurative work of Klimt. Cauchie was not in fact an architect but a mural painter, whose work graces many of Brussels' art nouveau buildings. The façade of his own house is strictly rectilinear (only the second-storey circular window is a certain mark of art nouveau), with minor decorative flourishes in the ironwork and the concrete bands. But the large figurative sgraffito panels display Cauchie's best art nouveau style. ☐

Adolphe Stoclet house 1905-11

9 | 279 avenue de Tervueren
Woluwe-Saint-Pierre, Brussels

architect
Josef Hoffmann

The giant, asymmetric forms of the Stoclet house, frequently known as the Palais Stoclet because of its scale, mark one of the key transitional buildings of the twentieth century. The design has many clear antecedents — Mackintosh, Otto Wagner, Olbrich — yet it looks forward to both art deco and the Modernists' explorations of form. The house is finished in white marble slabs that create a smooth, visibly hard surface, but the whole is framed by gilded metal borders. The free-flowing spaces and planes Hoffmann uses throughout the house, in fact, are always sharply defined by decorative borders. The smooth surfaces of marble are broken at points by various elements: the two-storey stair-hall, the concave curve of the garden façade. In an extremely modern way, however, Hoffmann's windows barely disrupt the wall plane, but seem merely last-minute cut-outs. The interior of the Stoclet house is a magnificent <u>Gesamtkunstwerk:</u> Hoffmann and the artists and craftsmen of the Wiener Werkstätte designed and built all the furniture, tableware, china, glass, door handles, etc. Most extraordinary is the dining-room with Hoffmann's characteristic black and white mosaic tiles around the edge of the floor and Gustav Klimt's iridescent mosaics adorning the marble walls. Despite the strongly Viennese character of the Stoclet house, in the dining-room in particular the influence of Mackintosh's 1901 design for an art-lover's house can clearly be seen. ☐

Hallet house 1906

10	346 avenue Louise Brussels	architect Victor Horta

The Hallet house is interesting primarily as a comparison with the slightly earlier Solvay house ◇ 2, also by Horta, a short way up the avenue Louise. In the few years between these two houses, of fairly similar size, Horta's style has become far more restrained, the decoration stripped down. Where before Horta seemed loath to leave the slightest area of the façade free of decorative flourishes, in the Hallet house the elegant curves of the windows are offset by the plain, flat stone niches on the first floor. Horta's previous exuberance is only hinted at in the flowing lines of the balcony ironwork. Yet another shift in his style is the complete detachment of ironwork ornamentation from stone structure: in the Solvay house the two were carefully integrated, in his own house and studio (built between the Solvay and Hallet houses) both were ornamented but independent. One of the curiosities of the Hallet house can be seen from the garden: the first floor glazed conservatory with its three glass domes, supported on three slender cast-iron columns.
☐

House 1907

11	17 place Antoine Delporte Saint-Gilles, Brussels	architect Paul Hamesse

Hamesse's house on place Delporte is one of Brussels' most successful works of art nouveau: shapes and decoration are kept in a fine compositional balance. Taking advantage of a crescent of houses, Hamesse split the design into two parts, so the house turns through part of the crescent. The tall casing containing the door emphasises the verticality of the house, but this is partially offset by the changing, bulging shapes of the windows above: on the first floor shield-shaped, on the second floor a rounded T-shape and at the top, a tiny pentagram. The disjunction these variations create is well balanced by the relative restraint of the other half. Here each window is similar in shape, but the treatment of the façade varies slightly. As with any fine art nouveau work, Hamesse devoted considerable attention to even small details: the iron door handle is of particular note. The relatively late date of this art nouveau house is reflected in its restrained decoration, but the jostling of elements, the unstable equilibrium of the parts, places it equal to the more famous buildings of several years earlier by Horta and others.
☐

Jespers studio 1928

12 | 149 avenue du Prince Héritier Brussels | **architect** Victor Bourgeois

In 1926, Bourgeois completed his Cité Moderne ◇1, where the major influence was Frank Lloyd Wright. In the Jespers studio, only two years later, Bourgeois designed one of the most visually Modern works in Brussels: the white, unadorned stucco, the plain strips of steel-framed windows show Bourgeois had switched his allegiance to Le Corbusier (who built the Guiette house in Antwerp in 1926). It took several years for Bourgeois' uncompromising interpretation of Modern movement architecture to find imitators in Brussels.
☐

Prévoyance Sociale building 1932

13 | 31 square de l'Aviation Anderlecht, Brussels | **architect** Maxime Brunfaut

The most remarkable feature of the Prévoyance Sociale building is the <u>Moderne</u> entrance lobby that has survived completely unaltered. All the elements of the <u>Moderne</u>, the successor to art deco, are intact: the double-height lobby, the curving, ship-like windows, the aluminium-clad columns, the open lift shaft, the mosaic marble floor, the views up the stairwells. If the calendar on the central counter had a year on it, most would agree it should be perpetually 1932.
☐

Berteaux house 1937

14 59 avenue du Fort Jaco
Brussels

architect
Louis Herman De Koninck

De Koninck is best known as Belgium's leading rationalist architect, with a number of notable works in the twenties that advanced the use of concrete shell construction. But his Berteaux house, with its overt nautical imagery, is probably his most likeable work. The emphasis on structure that De Koninck used in all of his works is here mediated by the playful use of three portholes, the rounded, almost streamlined corner, the large smokestack and the promenade deck on top.
☐

Social zone for the medical faculties 1969-82

15 Catholic University of Louvain
Woluwe-Saint-Lambert

architect
Lucien Kroll

Kroll, along with Ralph Erskine, is probably the most interesting of the contemporary group of architects who view architecture as a collective, democratic process. His work in Woluwe-Saint-Lambert, which includes housing, offices, dining-halls, shops, schools and a metro station, is the best illustration of his method. Kroll was selected as architect for the social zone in 1969 by a student group opposed to the Modern movement scheme originally proposed by university authorities. Kroll assumed the role of consultant, rather than authoritarian architect, and organised groups of students to develop the scheme. Kroll then worked out the necessary technical details to translate the student's concepts into buildings. As with all of his works, Kroll also involved construction workers in the working out of particular details, much as the master builders of the medieval cathedrals left detailed decoration to individual craftsmen. In the Alma metro station, for example, workmen

were responsible for the design of the decorative mosaic and the organic form of the ceiling.

Throughout the work, particularly in the early student housing, a goal was to create buildings that could easily be transformed as user requirements changed. As a result, short-life, atypical materials are frequently used: a staircase is made from scaffolding, corrugated metal is used as cladding in the patchwork composition of the façade. The product is an invigorating contrast to the banal, mediocre university buildings of the surroundings, but some of the details of Kroll's work are unfortunately weathering badly. Perhaps the enthusiasm that originally fuelled the students of 1969 has dissipated to such an extent that details that were meant to be changed in a few years have been left to corrode out of neglect and apathy.
☐

the Faber GUIDE

to twentieth-century ARCHITECTURE

Denmark

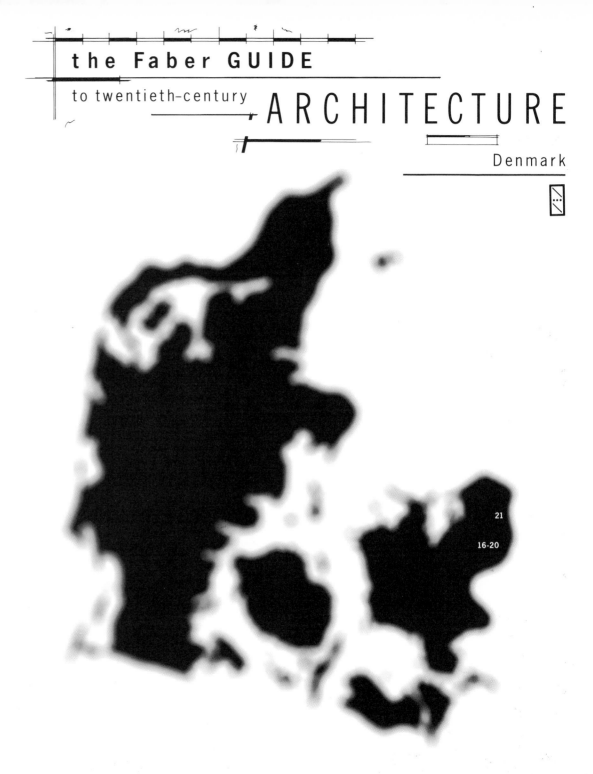

21

16-20

Church 1978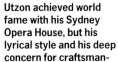

Jørn Utzon

16

Utzon achieved world fame with his Sydney Opera House, but his lyrical style and his deep concern for craftsmanship are well displayed in his church near Copenhagen. The opera house responds to the spectacular setting; faced with an anonymous suburban site, next to a highway intersection, Utzon's church turns in on itself, looking inwards into courtyards and the interior. Like many of Utzon's works, this is a work of exposed concrete and wood, with few other materials. The plan is extraordinarily simple, with roof-lit corridors running straight down the sides and the roughly square spaces opening off these corridors. It is in section that Utzon lets his imagination play, for sinuous concrete vaults form the ceilings of the church, chapel and the offices. The roof, in distinct contrast, is straight aluminium decking. While Utzon's opera house makes an expansive exterior statement, his Bagsvaerd church conceals its delights inside. □

Hector's House (now Metropol theatre) 1907

architect
Anton Rosen

17

A rare surviving example of a large-scale <u>Jugendstil</u> building. Originally a department store, Hector's House has now been partially converted into a theatre. Externally, however, it still retains more of the air of Secessionist Vienna than Copenhagen. Above the ground floor (which has been made unrecognisable through alterations) the strange half-columns are capped by floral garlands and seemingly organic drainspouts. The recessed third storey has a balcony running the length of the building.
☐

Grundtvigs church and housing 1913-40

architect
P. V. Jensen-Klint

18

The basic form of the Grundtvigs church is that of a Danish country church, but this traditional form is utterly transformed by the soaring abstracted gable façade, a combination of National Romantic and Expressionist styles. The church, of grand scale, is surrounded by small-scale houses whose portals repeat the church's façade motif, and the whole is of brick and tile. Jensen-Klint, who originally trained as a painter, was a passionate believer in the importance of the vernacular, as well as the importance of craftsmanship. Yet he despised those architects who mimicked the past: his goal was to revive in new form the spirit of the old architecture. His belief in craftsmanship extended to his preferred title of master mason (<u>bygmester</u>) rather than architect.
☐

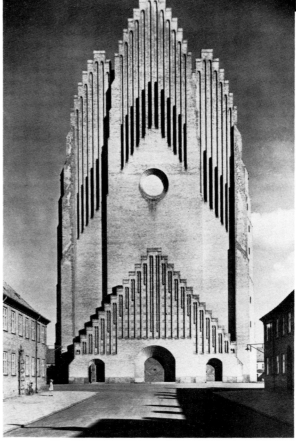

Police headquarters 1919-24

architect

Hack Kampmann

19

Most of Kampmann's work was eclectic, for example his Aarhus national library (1898-1902), which combined elements of Labrouste and Burges. But in his final work, the police headquarters, he became the most severe of Classicists. The headquarters is on a roughly triangular site, and to passers-by the building presents high, unadorned, forbidding walls. But inside, Kampmann allows more open gestures: an imposing circular courtyard, surrounded by an arcade of paired Doric columns, acts as counterpoint to a smaller, but still monumental, square court with giant order Corinthian columns. The interior borrows Classical details from a wide range of sources: Michelangelo, Palladio, C. F. Hansen, etc. Perhaps the most remarkable detail is the giant scallop-shaped 'keystone' over the director's door (designed by Holger Jacobsen, one of Kampmann's associates).
☐

Strandvejen
Hellerup

Tuborg administration building 1914-15

architect

Anton Rosen

While some of Rosen's early work showed signs of <u>Jugendstil</u> influence, the dominant strain in his buildings is the National Romantic movement. The Tuborg administration building appears from the outside a fairly conventional Danish work of the nineteenth or perhaps late eighteenth century: steep mansard roofs, Classical composition, traditional materials. The weightiness of the architecture, however, sets it apart from earlier works: the way the building seems to have almost sunk into the ground. Chunky structural half-columns between the windows thrust downwards, making the ground-level brick buttresses a visual necessity. Inside, the building is arranged around a double-height covered court with spare decoration.

☐

20

Gammel Strandvej 13
Humleboek

Louisiana museum 1958, 1968, 1978-80

architect

Bo and Wohlert

21

The Louisiana museum is the supreme achievement of Danish design in the fifties: a series of low, simple pavilions disposed sympathetically in the landscape with magnificent views over the Oresund. White-washed brick walls contrast with the large expanses of glass walls. The roof is supported on timber beams. Jørgen Bo describes the museum best: 'A covered walk through a varied garden where the plan of the building expresses the rise and fall of the ground, and where large windows deliberately frame picturesque landscape topics, resulting in an unbroken dialogue between nature and art.' Bo's work is characterised by this sensitivity to nature, but the Louisiana extends the concept further than in other buildings. The interrelationship between the architecture and

the art is also finely observed, especially the room where the spindly Giacometti sculptures are mimicked by the thin wood screens of the interior. After the museum opened in 1958, Bo and Wohlert designed two extensions in 1968 and 1978-80 in a similar style.

☐

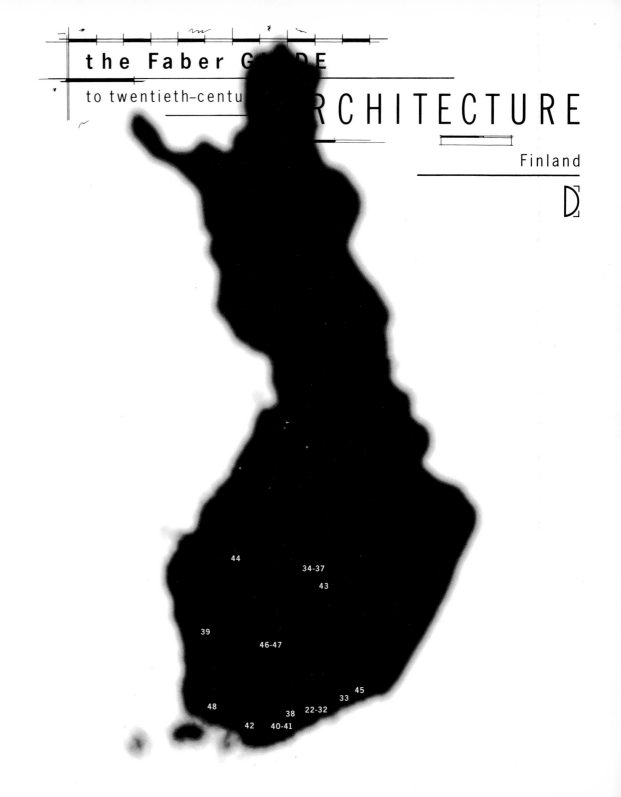

the Faber GUIDE

to twentieth-centu RCHITECTURE

Finland

D

44

34-37

43

39

46-47

45

33

48

38   22-32

42   40-41

Pohjola Insurance Company building 1899-1902

architect

Herman Gesellius, Armas Lindgren and Eliel Saarinen

*Aleksantrinkatu 44
Helsinki*

The Pohjola building was the first by Gesellius, Lindgren and Saarinen in the National Romantic style, and as such it was one of the key works in the development of the style. The rock-faced squared rubble that clads the Pohjola building was to become one of the identifying marks of National Romanticism, particularly under Lars Sonck, but it was Pohjola that first established the technique. A large five-storey building on a corner of Helsinki's principal shopping street, the Pohjola is a composition in three parts: the first two floors are of very roughly hewn ashlar, above are two floors of slightly less rusticated stone, and the top floor is of virtually smooth surface. The stone-carved decoration is naturalistic and at times humorous. The entrance is flanked by paired columns surmounted by tree-like branches and vegetation that climbs across the top of the surround. Carved animals in turn rest on this outgrowth in a symmetrical composition. The main rooms of the interior, notably the first-floor boardroom, are similarly richly decorated. The winding spiral staircase that climbs up from the entrance hall, with its intricately carved posts, is particularly inventive.

□

National Museum 1902-10

architect

Herman Gesellius, Armas Lindgren and Eliel Saarinen

*Mannerheimintie 34
Helsinki*

The National Museum is not the best work of Gesellius, Lindgren and Saarinen during their fertile early years together, but in its rather eclectic style and composition it makes an intriguing comparison with their more strongly National Romantic works like the Pohjola building ◇ 22.
The massive base of squared granite rubble is topped by a virtually unadorned stucco. The grouping and forms of the museum have strong ecclesiastical overtones. The most striking aspect of the design, however, is the tall tower topped by alternating layers of red brick and copper roofs. The minimal decoration, though not as rich as in the Pohjola building, is again naturalistic.

□

Telephone company building 1903-5

architect
Lars Sonck

Korkeavuorenkatu 35
Helsinki

The telephone company building is Sonck's finest civic work in his early National Romantic style, and it makes an interesting comparison with the slightly earlier Pohjola Insurance building ◇ 22 by Gesellius, Lindgren and Saarinen. As with the Pohjola building, Sonck's is a progression of massive layers: the base of ashlar is surmounted by rock-faced squared rubble. Sonck emphasises the contrast in textures, notably through the smooth ashlar of the gabled door surround and the stubby, smooth columns of the second-floor windows. The red tiles which originally clad the roof have unfortunately been replaced by copper. The building is planned around a courtyard, but its principal interest lies in its truly massive forms, which far exceed those used in the Pohjola building. Perhaps the only other architect who used rough stone in such a massive, contrasting manner was the Philadelphian Frank Furness. □

Train station 1904-14

architect

Saarinen and Gesellius

Rautatientori
Helsinki

Saarinen and Gesellius' design for Helsinki's central train station won a competition in 1904, but in the six years before building began, Saarinen, using some of the competition prize money, travelled through Germany, Austria and Britain. It is possibly in these journeys that the influence of Vienna imposed itself on the original design. The main façade is symmetrical with a large rounded arch, recalling the gable fingers of Olbrich's wedding tower in Darmstadt, flanked by giant paired column/statues that hold globe lights. The tower, with its Viennese distorted Classicism, is placed asymmetrically to one side. Inside, the main concourse features an exposed concrete vault, innovatory at the time. The large complex is one of the few twentieth-century train stations – Bonatz's in Stuttgart is perhaps the only one of comparable stature – that communicates the excitement, the grandeur of train travel.

□

Stock exchange 1910-11

architect
Lars Sonck

*Fabianinkatu 14
Helsinki*

The stock exchange is the last of Sonck's major works, although his career continued until the 1940s. In the stock exchange, the strong National Romanticism of his earlier works has given way to a more restrained Classicism. The façade is symmetrical, with pilaster-like piers crowned by almost Viennese wreaths. The ground floor, in contrast, has the rounded Richardsonian Romanesque arches Sonck used in his earlier works, but the stone here is smooth, pared away in comparison with the heavy entrance of the telephone company building, for instance. The offices are grouped around an open courtyard with a glazed roof. The entrance to the stock exchange itself is from this court-yard, by a ceremonial, open, double flight of steps.
☐

Käpylä garden city 1920-5

architect
Martti Välikangas

*Pohjolankatu
Käpylä, Helsinki*

Käpylä garden city is one of the best examples of the garden city movement that developed originally in Britain. The basic concept of the garden city, as originally outlined by Ebenezer Howard in his 1892 Tomorrow. A Peaceful Path to Reform (better known by its 1902 title Garden Cities of Tomorrow), was to inter-weave housing, public facilities and parkland to create an almost rural urban environment. At Käpylä Välikangas did this with consummate skill. The detached, semidetached and terraced houses are of simple, traditional construction and form, but enlivened with the sparest, most primitive Classical details: thin wooden Doric columns, wooden cornices, friezes and scrolls. The houses are grouped around large communal gardens, parks and recreational facilities in large squares barred to automobiles, and are connected by plank fences and arcades. Although the planning is formal – squares, crescents and circuses predominate – the rich planting of trees and plants throughout does create Howard's ideal of a garden city.
☐

Own house 1934-6

architect
Alvar Aalto

Riihitie 20
Munkkiniemi, Helsinki

The house he designed for himself marks one of Aalto's first decisive breaks with a pure, functionalist style. The house is composed of a series of interlocking cubic volumes, but the surface treatment of these volumes betrays Aalto's deviation from unadorned Modernism. The structure is of tubular steel filled with concrete, with exterior walls of whitewashed brick. The brick is left exposed on the ground floor and on the upper storey of the western façade, where Aalto had his studio. But the more private areas of the house have their exterior walls clad in clear-finished birch.

□

National Pensions Institute 1952-6

architect
Alvar Aalto

Keskuskatu 3
Helsinki

Aalto won the competition for the National Pensions Institute in 1948, but the eventual building was constructed on a different site. In a crowded business area of Helsinki, the institute is a large office building for 800 employees. The distinct, red-brick cubic masses of offices are grouped around a raised inner garden court which provides both natural light and relative quiet. The most interesting feature of the institute is the triple-height central hall, which was used for interviewing pensioners. Large triangular roof-lights flood the hall with natural light. Exposing the services above the roof-lights, although now commonplace, was at the time innovatory.

□

30

Own studio 1953-6

architect

Alvar Aalto

Riihitie
Munkkiniemi, Helsinki

Aalto's white brick studio, on the same street as his house of twenty years earlier, consists of two large drafting rooms, each with its own reception area, archives and a conference room. The roughly L-shaped building surrounds a courtyard, which has been landscaped into an amphitheatre for lectures, social occasions and recreation. No windows overlook the street, reducing outside disturbance, although the street itself is very quiet. The amphitheatre, now rather overgrown, is defined by the concave curve of the double-height studio's south wall. This south wall also curves upward, creating a dramatically shaped interior space.

□

31

Temppeliaukio church 1960-9

architect

Timo Suomalainen

Lutherinkatu 3
Helsinki

Built on an open rock outcrop surrounded by apartment buildings, the design for the Temppeliaukio church was centred around the need to preserve the rock. So the church is cut into the bedrock, and the striking interior is created by the exposed, unfinished rock face. The effect is heightened by the sensitive, simple use of materials for the design: everything is of stone, concrete or copper. The bedrock walls are topped by a rough course of boulders, which provides the base for the radiating concrete fins that support the swirling dome of beaten copper.
□

32

Finlandia Hall 1962-75

architect

Alvar Aalto

Mannerheimintie 13
Helsinki

Finlandia Hall, a combined concert hall and conference centre, was intended as part of the redevelopment of Helsinki's Töölö Bay area. Aalto was involved in the plans for the entire redevelopment, but Finlandia Hall is virtually the only aspect that was ever built. The reinforced concrete framework is faced in white marble, a material Aalto reserved for cultural buildings in his later works, and black granite. The internal volumes are all expressed on the outside: a flat base housing lobbies, offices and ancillary facilities supports the fan-shaped halls. Seen from across the bay, the rear wall of the main concert hall is articulated by three seating banks, recalling the 1927 Moscow Tram Workers' Club by Konstantin Melnikov. Aalto's special skill, however, is in the immaculate detailing throughout the complex: the marble and blue-painted birchwood in the main auditorium, the leather twisted around the bronze handrails (one of Aalto's signatures), the indirect lighting reflecting off brass-lined surfaces. The overall planning has not been neglected, however. Separate entrances can be provided for the two halls and the smaller conference rooms, and the foyers that serve each can be closed off for independent use. □

33

Vuoksenniska church 1956-9

architect

Alvar Aalto

Vuoksenniska
Imatra

In contrast to many of Aalto's works in Finland, Vuoksenniska church is not secluded in the midst of a pine forest, but sits in the middle of an industrial area of Imatra. The tall, abstract bell-tower, topped by a large cross, marks the religious centre as distinct from the numerous factory chimneys. The irregular form of the church itself is determined by a pair of rolling acoustic partitions (of 40-cm-thick concrete) inside. These partitions enable the church to be used for social as well as religious activities. With the partitions in position, an intimate church for a congregation of 290 is formed, but with the partitions open, 800 persons can be accommodated. The plan was partially determined by the Lutheran liturgy: the wall on the pulpit side is straight, and the opposite wall, for acoustic reasons, is in three curved sections (the sections created by the partitions). The church is also vertically asymmetric, with the windows along the curving walls placed in sloping diagonals. With the fan-shaped ceiling, the windows act as an acoustic reflecting board. □

34

Workers' Club 1923-5

architect

Alvar Aalto

Väinönkatu 7
Jyväskylä

Aalto's building for the Jyväskylä Labour Association was his first important public work. The stripped Classicism of the Workers' Club can be seen as Aalto's reaction against the decorative excesses of National Romanticism. The club consisted of a double-storey assembly hall and theatre over a ground-floor restaurant and circular café. The ground floor has unfortunately been completely altered. The unusual shape of the café derived from Aalto's need to support the weight of the theatre (which seats 300) and avoid a maze of columns. The lighter weight of the stage was supported by a rectilinear grid of columns in the restaurant.

The exterior was conditioned by the internal demands. So the upper storeys are blind walls with minimal fenestration and a grand balcony at the front that opens on to the foyer. The curious balcony window is a Palladian window in reverse with a rectangular central window flanked by round-arched side windows. The ground floor, in contrast, is completely glazed between its short Doric columns. Although much of Aalto's decoration has been lost, his door handles have survived: this detail, and concern for handrails, can be seen in buildings throughout Aalto's career.

☐

35

University of Jyväskylä 1951-7

architect

Alvar Aalto

Seminaarinkatu 15
Jyväskylä

In 1951 Aalto won a limited competition for the expansion of the then Jyväskylä Teachers' Training College. Aalto's red-brick buildings form a U-shaped group around a park and sports field. The main building, which contains offices, classrooms and a library, is at the base of the 'U', acting as the pivot and as an end stop for the main road entrance. A large foyer opens out with views through full-height glass walls to woods and Lake Jyväsjärvi. The foyer actually lies partially under the grand fan-shaped auditorium. To the other side of the foyer lies a triple-height stairway hall lit by Aalto's characteristic roof-lights, which acts as the main pedestrian route to other parts of the building. The rear wall of the main building, together with the dense pine trees, forms an outdoor courtyard, more naturalistic than the one at Otaniemi ◇ 40. The east side of the 'U' is formed by the staff meeting-room, the student refectory and the students' hall of residence (now the language department). Behind this group is Aalto's 1964 student union building. The staff meeting-room, which Aalto named Lyhty (lantern), is a simple temple-like framework of white-painted concrete and large windows. Terrace walls link it to the students' refectory. The refectory itself has a wooden beam ceiling and clerestory windows along the central court side and full-height windows facing the woods to the east. The north end of the 'U' is closed by a demonstration school and its associated buildings. The school is linked to the main building by the main library, which has a sunken reading room lit from the roof, an idea Aalto first used in his 1927 library in Viipuri (now Viborg USSR). A covered path, under the first storey overhang of the buildings, also connects the two. On the west side of the 'U' are a gymnasium and swimming hall overlooking the sports field. The white physical education building, further along this end of the 'U', is a 1970 addition by A. Sipinen.

☐

Administrative and cultural centre 1964-?

architect
Alvar Aalto

*Hannikaisenkatu 17
Jyväskylä*

Like most of Aalto's town centre designs, that for Jyväskylä is grouped around a 'citizens' square.' The square itself is a continuation of a pedestrian path from the town's Kirkkopuisto (church square) through to Lake Jyväsjärvi; Aalto's square is disposed so a through visual connection is also made. A tower, yet to be built, containing the council chamber, is intended to dominate the square, as the council chamber dominates the much smaller centre at nearby Säynätsalo. On the sloping site, the police headquarters (completed 1970), with its curvilinear concrete wall hiding its car park, anchors the bottom north end. Next to this, on the bottom edge of the site, is the building department office (completed posthumously in 1978). The theatre (also completed posthumously in 1981) is a fan-shaped design, with both a traditional proscenium-arch auditorium and a small theatre/recital hall. The theatre design suffers from its long history, but preserved from Aalto's original conception is the low, enclosed entrance hall with a double-height foyer above with large windows looking over both the Kirkkopuisto and the citizens' square. As in the Aalto Museum ◇ 37, the façade is given visual texture by the vertical ceramic rods fixed to the light-coloured brick.
□

Alvar Aalto Museum 1971-3

architect
Alvar Aalto

*Seminaarinkatu 7
Jyväskylä*

Few architects can have the chance to design a museum for themselves, but such was the stature that Aalto had in Finland, and in particular in Jyväskylä where he started his career, that in 1966 the Alvar Aalto Museum was founded. In 1970, the museum society asked Aalto to design a home for the museum, which is one of the jewels of his late work. Aalto himself was somewhat opposed to the idea of the museum: 'I don't think a one-man museum is reasonable. It will soon become cold and dead. This museum shall be a living one where the pictorial art and architecture are represented from various sides.'
A pale brick building on a sloping site, the exterior of the museum is distinguished by the raking rows of roof-lights. The brick walls are given visual texture with vertical ceramic rods and metal louvres. Inside, the lower floor consists of a hall and café, as well as offices, storage rooms and workshop accommodation. The exhibition hall is on the main floor, lit by roof-lights. The ceiling slopes upwards to the rear wall with its undulating panels, a reference to Aalto's 1938 New York World Fair pavilion. The museum is next door to Aalto's Museum of Central Finland (1959-61).
□

Hvitträsk 1902

architect
Herman Gesellius, Armas Lindgren and Eliel Saarinen

Kirkkonummi

Outside Helsinki, on a steep hillside overlooking a lake, Gesellius, Lindgren and Saarinen built their tiny colony of houses and studios, pursuing the Arts and Crafts ideal. The houses are grouped picturesquely around a central courtyard, with terraced gardens at either end. The ground floors are built out of partially stuccoed boulders, so the houses seem to grow out of the ground. Above this the houses are shingled, and the plan constantly breaks out into window bays. The whole is capped by steep, sweeping pantiled roofs. The three partners originally collaborated on Hvitträsk, but when Lindgren left the partnership in 1905 and Gesellius in 1907, Saarinen had the complex to himself until he emigrated to the United States in 1923. Saarinen is responsible for most of the interiors, which he altered to his taste: particularly remarkable are the large tile-faced fireplaces adorned with copper and iron embellishments. The treatment of space, with its changes of level and the open, flowing circulation between rooms, is similar to the roughly contemporary work of Frank Lloyd Wright in his prairie style houses.
□

39

Villa Mairea 1937-8

architect
Alvar Aalto

Noormarkku (near Pori)

Harry and Maire Gullichsen, who commissioned Aalto for the Sunila cellulose factory ◇ 45, also gave him the opportunity to design his domestic masterpiece, the Villa Mairea. An L-shaped house, basically built out of rectangular volumes, it stands in the midst of a pine forest at the top of a hill. The view out is of unbroken stretches of forest, with glimpses of a river and sawmill. The house, with its sauna wing reaching out on one side, is built around an inner court with a kidney-shaped pool next to the sauna. The dense pine forest creates an effective 'wall' to enclose the open side of this court. But this bare description fails to do justice to Aalto's conception, for it is in the constant attention to detail that he created his masterwork. The rectilinear volumes of the house are augmented by the free-flowing forms throughout: the kidney-shaped pool, the piano-shaped entrance porch and the rounded trapezoidal first-floor studio. Aalto's use of wood for most of the details draws the house and forest together. His invention with wood is unsurpassed. The entrance canopy is supported on natural wood poles, lashed together as by a frontiersman; steel pipe columns are wrapped together in pairs with caning; polished grains are set against rough finishes; wall cladding and balconies use wood in subtly different ways. Aalto did not neglect other aspects in the design. Sunlight is regulated on the exterior of the large windows with external venetian blinds, and small bedroom windows are slanted away from the rising sun so the very early light of Finnish summers can be avoided. The plan of the villa is reminiscent of the work of Frank Lloyd Wright, with a free flow of spaces in a pinwheel arrangement. The extension of the house, through a covered walkway (the roof is grassed), to the sauna wing pulls the interior of the house into the surrounding nature.
□

Dipoli congress and student centre 1964-6

architect
Reima Pietilä

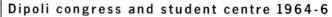

Jämeräntaival
Otaniemi

Pietilä is a rarity: a modern-day Expressionist. The Dipoli centre, his best work, stands on a rocky outcrop amid dense woods. The building seems to grow out of this context, with the boulders of the site forming the base of the centre. The plan is divided into two parts, with a functional, rectilinear half for offices and administrative areas, while the public rooms follow the dynamic lines of the site. The external cladding of the concrete structure is copper sheet, but in areas where the concrete has been left exposed, the board-markings have been left unaltered. The stone outcrop extends into the interior of the building in boulder-strewn walls along the windows. The concrete joists of the structure spread like a tree's branches, with the timber ceilings hung off them. The irregular plan serves to encircle parts of the landscape bringing the exterior visually into the interior.

☐

40

Institute of Technology 1961-4

architect
Alvar Aalto

Jämeräntaival
Otaniemi

Aalto designed the master plan for the Institute of Technology as the result of a competition he won, and the major buildings. The most interesting work in the complex is the group of administration and academic buildings dominated by the arc of the auditorium. The auditorium acts as the hinge for the group, with the administration office to the west and the main classroom blocks (arranged around courts), disposed to the east. This arrangement creates an outdoor court which Aalto exploits with his curving auditorium block: the roof of the auditorium is transformed into seats for an open-air theatre. The interior of the auditorium is dominated by the dramatic roof, with the arching steel structure slicing through and natural light pouring in from the roof-lights. All of Aalto's

buildings at the institute are clad in red brick, which gives them a common identity although the forms are quite different.

☐

42

Tuberculosis sanatorium 1929-33

architect

Alvar Aalto

Paimio

The 1928 competition for the Paimio sanatorium was the first major competition that Aalto won. His design combines elements of the so-called 'heroic' age of Modern architecture with his characteristic nuance in details. The layout and constructional details owe something to Johannes Duiker's Zonnestraal sanatorium (1926-8) ◇ 272, Hilversum, Holland, which Aalto saw in his travels in 1928. The various elements of the sanatorium are disposed so each has a rational orientation: the long, tall ward block enables every room to face south, the block which contains public rooms lies next to the kitchens and service facilities, the doctors' quarters are in row houses completely isolated from the main buildings, with no view of the sanatorium (to allow them to escape from work when at home). Aalto designed the furniture, lavatories, lights, ventilating systems, every element of the sanatorium. As always in his best work, the design derived from careful consideration of the users' needs. Feeling that the typical hospital interior takes no account of bed-ridden patients, Aalto set about developing a design that would improve the environment from the bed. So the ceiling in the two-bed rooms is painted a dark colour, except for a light area directly over the patients' heads. A light fitting just below this light-painted area sends a wash of light upwards. Similarly, Aalto provided a soft wall surface behind the beds, instead of the exposed hard walls found elsewhere.

☐

43

Town hall 1950-2

architect

Alvar Aalto

Valtterintie/Kirkkotie
Säynätsalo

Aalto's design for the Säynätsalo town hall won a competition in 1949. A rugged island with a population of only 3,000, Aalto's complex, which includes the council chamber and offices, together with a public library, gives a focus to the scattered dwellings. The tower-like red-brick council chamber rises symbolically high above the other parts, clustered around a courtyard as though they were part of a medieval castle. Brick steps lead up to the raised courtyard, where one enters either the offices and council chamber or the library. The courtyard, now picturesquely overgrown, has a tiny pool beside an office corridor: wooden posts march around the courtyard acting in places as glazing bars, elsewhere as supports for a pergola. The courtyard spills out at one end in an irregular-shaped grass terrace stairway, now sadly nearly overgrown.

The cubic council chamber is reached through a brick stair-passage lit by clerestory windows. Triangulated timber trusses support the secondary roof framing and are fully exposed, a fine example of Aalto's experimentation in the fifties with wood. The main level of the library (the lower level was originally shops) has a flood of light from the south-facing windows. The office corridor, overlooking the courtyard, is also south-facing.

☐

Alvar Aaltonkatu/Kirkkokatu
Seinäjoki

Civic centre 1952-85

architect

Alvar Aalto

Aalto's civic centre in Seinäjoki, now known as the Aalto Centre, is the most complete and best example of his urban design. Above this, each of the individual buildings must figure among Aalto's best work (something that could not be said, for example, of the individual elements of the Jyväskylä centre). The centre is the result of two competitions, one for the church in 1952, another for the administrative and cultural centre in 1959. Aalto, of course, won both competitions and created a unified ensemble over nearly twenty years of design and building (the theatre is expected to be completed posthumously in 1985, ten years after his death). Aalto's plan rigidly separates pedestrian and vehicular circulation: a paved esplanade stretches from the civic and cultural centre to the religious centre. Each building is differentiated both by colour and shape, but Aalto's rich vocabulary of details and textures makes their common identity unmistakable. The church (1952-60) has a narrow fan-shaped plan with high walls capped by a pyramidal roof. Adjoining the church is a parish hall (1964-6), which wraps around a terraced square. The square is used for open-air worship and large-scale celebrations and serves as a counterpoint to the civic square. This religious centre is marked by the towering cross of the belfry and clock tower (similar in conception to the tower of the

Vuoksenniska church ◇ 33). Across from the religious centre, and acting as a foil, is the startlingly blue town hall (1961-5), with its tall council chamber (the chamber, the symbolic centre of the democratic process, is always emphasised by Aalto). The dark-blue tiles of the exterior are arranged in a vertical pattern, but white courses create a distinct horizontal counterpoint. The council chamber stands completely free of the ground on pilotis, a rare reference by Aalto to Le Corbusier. The main entrance to the offices is in this space under the chamber, but the chamber itself can be entered on the main level via a staircase that climbs up its side. From this entrance, broad grass steps, with flowers and fountains on the side, fan out to the civic square.

The library (1963-5) sits opposite the town hall, with a long blank wall facing across the civic square. Offices, meeting rooms and small reading areas are in this front rectangular block, but the main reading-room and library stacks are in a fan-shaped hall that spreads out on the far side of the civic square. As in other Aalto libraries, a sunken reading area, isolated from the main stacks, is in the middle of the reading-room, radially aligned with the control desk. Natural light is provided by a clerestory full-length louvred window. The theatre closes off the far end of the civic square. Aalto intended it to be a compact, multi-purpose building which could also serve as a convention hall and clubhouse.

□

45

Cellulose factory and workers' housing 1935-9

architect

Alvar Aalto

Sunila (an island near Kotka)

The complex of industrial buildings and housing on Sunila was one of Aalto's first large-scale works. A result of the patronage of industrialists Harry and Maire Gullichsen, Aalto's design marks the beginning of his inter-weaving of architecture and nature. The enormous brick cubic forms of the factory are contrasted by the white-painted concrete storage shed, and the entire complex is embedded in the rough Baltic granite of the island. Aalto preserved the contours of the island: the production process moves from a naturally high level and steps down towards the harbour. The centre of the factory complex is built up into a terrace from which all phases of production can be observed. This central terrace area includes the administrative offices and laboratories, as well as functioning as a quiet garden separate from the noise of production. The various elements of the factory are connected by open, park-like paths, in which the original trees have been left standing.

Aalto's Modern-movement-style housing, across an inlet from the factory, was planned so only the south slopes contained housing, with the valleys serving as pathways and gardens. The pine forest on the north slopes remained undisturbed. Among the innovatory features of the housing are the staggered-layout town houses for supervisory staff with fan-shaped walled gardens, and the workers' terraces that use the slope of the site to create opposite-side entrances for upper and lower units and do away with stairs.

☐

46

Market hall 1901

architect

H. Åberg

Hämeenkatu 19
Tampere

Åberg's market hall is a particularly fine example of a public work in the National Romantic style. The hall itself is in the form of a basilica, with the central aisle lit by clerestory windows. Iron trusses support the roof, and vaguely <u>jugend</u> details are found on the main end-wall windows. The market stalls themselves are, however, the most interesting part of the work. Rigidly symmetrical bays with wood detailing in a folksy style, these stalls in the centre of Finland's second largest city demonstrate the National Romantic urge to find the picturesque everywhere.

☐

47

St John's church (Tampere cathedral) 1902-7

architect

Lars Sonck

*Tuomiokirkon puisto
Tampere*

Sonck's design for St John's won first prize in a competition of 1899-1900. He was working at the time on St Michael's in Turku, but it was with St John's that Sonck first fully expressed the National Romantic style: a blend, for Sonck, of neo-Gothic and <u>Jugendstil</u>. The form of the exterior looks like a fairly conventional neo-Gothic church, but Sonck has stripped away traditional historical details – there are no mouldings, capitals, tracery, etc. Instead, Sonck achieves his effects through the contrast of rough and smooth surfaces, and through the angular primitivism of the arches and spires. The church is clad in rock-faced squared granite, in various colours and of vastly different shapes and textures. The gateways and walls surrounding the church are constructed of undressed boulders. The interior belies the seemingly traditional form of the exterior, for Sonck's church has a centralised, rather than directional, plan. A 16-metre-square star vault arches over the interior. Balconies on almost flat segmental arches enclose the space. The frescoes, in the Finnish medieval tradition, are by Hugo Simberg and Magnus Enckell. □

48

St Michael's church 1894-1905

architect

Lars Sonck

*Puistokatu 16
Turku*

Sonck won the competition for St Michael's at the age of twenty-four, in his last year as a student. But it was not for another five years, until 1899, that construction work began on the church. By that time, Sonck's style had gone through a transformation to the beginnings of National Romanticism. The church council insisted, however, that the church be built in its competition form so Sonck's modifications were confined to detail. St Michael's is based on the north-German neo-Gothic of the late-nineteenth century, but Sonck rejected the rich decoration of the German churches. Mouldings are done away with, and carved stone decoration is of local ferns, horse chestnuts and varieties of fungi. The roughly hewn stone that was to become characteristic of Sonck is absent in this early work: surfaces are of smooth brickwork. The interior plan is fairly conventional, but the balconies on three sides rest on low segmental arches that anticipate the brooding, almost claustrophobic atmosphere of Sonck's St John's church in Tampere ◇ 47.
The painted decoration, by Max Frelander, reveals the affinity between the National Romantic style and Viennese Secessionism. □

the Faber GUIDE

to twentieth-century ARCHITECTURE

France

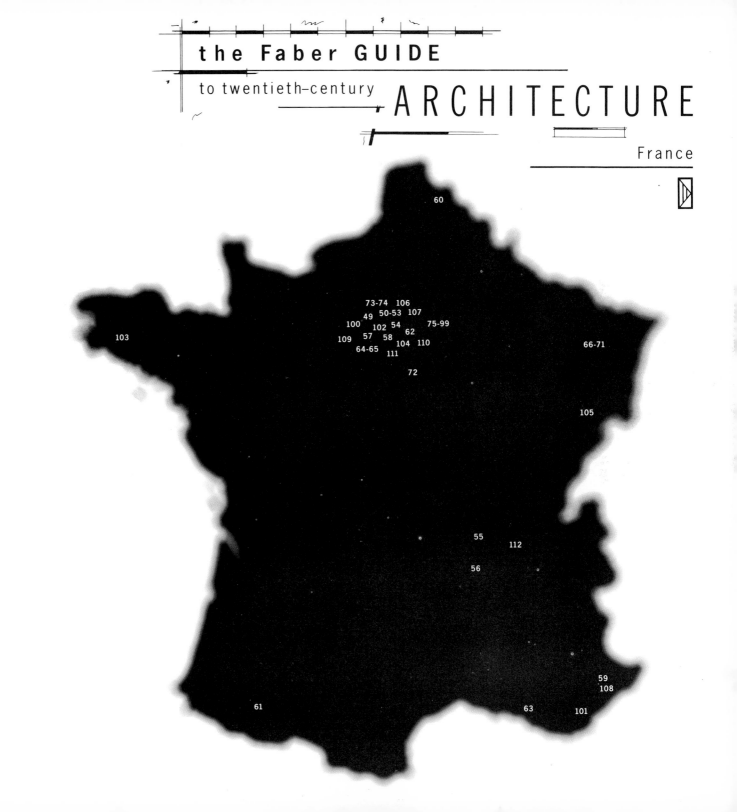

Clinic 1977-80

21 rue de Sartrouville
Bézons

49

Jean Nouvel, one of the most versatile French architects of the eighties, is a rare French practitioner of High-Tech architecture. But where the English masters of High-Tech tend to be serious and pragmatic, Nouvel often seems to design with tongue firmly in cheek. His clinic, an addition to rather banal older buildings, refers to the passion the early Modern movement had for boats, trains and automobiles. The design resembles the top decks of an ocean liner, sliced off and planted in the ground: the smooth and corrugated aluminium panels are visibly riveted together, gangways lead to the entrance, steel balconies and railings encircle the decks. The imagery is decidely nautical; the details are not executed for only functional reasons. Particularly fine is the chequerboard tile pattern that snakes around the clinic, defining its plinth.

☐

House 1905

11 rue Denfert-Rochereau
Boulogne-Billancourt

50

A good example of the rustic style of art nouveau architecture, all the more interesting because of the two nearby Le Corbusier houses that make such a striking contrast. The supreme example of this rustic style was Hector Guimard's Castle Henriette, Sèvres (1899-1900), which was unfortunately demolished in 1969. This small house in Boulogne-Billancourt, however, shares many of the characteristics: a basic structure of rough rubble (like parts of the wall of Castel Béranger ◇ 77), typically exuberant ironwork, and the curiously discordant, homely touch of the wooden gable.

☐

Le Corbusier

Lipschitz and Miestschaninoff houses 1924

7-9 allée les Pins
Boulogne-Billancourt

51

These twin houses are characteristic of Le Corbusier's early Modern houses, but they have perhaps the most nautical feeling of any. The ground floor contains the artists' double-height studios with their large window walls. The proper first floor, therefore, is no more than stairways and storage (Le Corbusier in fact called this floor the middle floor) and the second floor becomes the living area. Of particular interest, given the way he developed the theme throughout his career, is the footbridge that connects the two houses: thirty years later in Chandigarh, India, the footbridge reappears to connect on a grand scale the secretariat and the parliament buildings.
☐

Le Corbusier

Cook house 1926

6 rue Denfert-Rochereau
Boulogne-Billancourt

52

The Cook house is the first built work to demonstrate all of Le Corbusier's 'five points of the new architecture': <u>pilotis</u>, roof gardens, free plan, horizontal window strip and a free façade. In both plan and elevation, the Cook house is almost an exact square; Le Corbusier called it 'la vraie maison cubique'. The ground floor is almost entirely open to the garden and contains the garage and entrance hall. The first floor, traditionally a <u>piano nobile</u> for public rooms, is used instead for the bedrooms and bathrooms. On this floor, Le Corbusier exploits the absence of load-bearing walls, and uses free-flowing partitions to create a variety of curved, free spaces. The second floor contains the double-height living-room, the dining-room and kitchen. The top floor has the open terrace, with its characteristic 'cornice' framing views over the Bois de Boulogne, and a small library.
☐

City hall 1931-5

avenue André Morizet
Boulogne-Billancourt

53

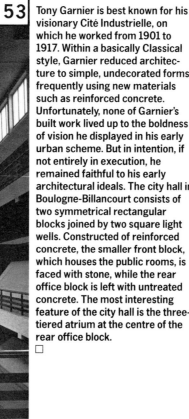

Tony Garnier is best known for his visionary Cité Industrielle, on which he worked from 1901 to 1917. Within a basically Classical style, Garnier reduced architecture to simple, undecorated forms, frequently using new materials such as reinforced concrete. Unfortunately, none of Garnier's built work lived up to the boldness of vision he displayed in his early urban scheme. But in intention, if not entirely in execution, he remained faithful to his early architectural ideals. The city hall in Boulogne-Billancourt consists of two symmetrical rectangular blocks joined by two square light wells. Constructed of reinforced concrete, the smaller front block, which houses the public rooms, is faced with stone, while the rear office block is left with untreated concrete. The most interesting feature of the city hall is the three-tiered atrium at the centre of the rear office block.

□

Maison du Peuple (central market) 1938-9

boulevard du Général-Leclerc
Clichy

54

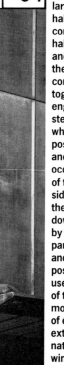

The Maison du Peuple consists of a large market hall, public meeting hall, and can also be used for concerts and theatre. The market hall is used during the daytime, and is converted to other uses in the evenings. To facilitate this conversion, Beaudouin & Lods, together with the pioneering engineer Jean Prouvé, designed a steel frame and panel construction where as many elements as possible could be easily moved and replaced. The market hall occupies the entire ground floor of the site, with a gallery on three sides. For the evening conversions, the balustrade of the gallery folds down, and the open well is closed by sections of floor. These floor panels are stored during the day and are mechanically moved into position to form the floor. When used as a cinema, the central part of the first floor is enclosed by movable partitions. Vertical strips of enamelled steel clad the exterior of the hall, and filtered natural light is let in through glass windows backed with translucent fluted plastic.

□

Monastery of Sainte-Marie-de-la-Tourette 1956-9

Départementale 19
Eveux-sur-Arbresle

55

With the pilgrimage chapel at Ronchamp ◇105, the monastery of La Tourette is one of the great works of Le Corbusier's late career. But while Ronchamp is exuberant and welcoming, a beacon on its hill, La Tourette is reclusive and austere. Le Corbusier received the commission for La Tourette from Father Alain Couturier, one of the more progressive Dominican priests. At Couturier's suggestion, Le Corbusier visited the twelfth-century abbey of Le Thoronet to understand the monastic life. In the standard Dominican monastery programme of church, oratory, refectory, atrium, chapter room, lecture rooms, library and cells, Le Corbusier endowed La Tourette with the spirit of the order: the rough materials, the simplicity of form, suggest a rejection of worldly things and encourage the intense pursuit of the religious life.

La Tourette is organised around a central court, with the large, blank box of the church dominating one side. Visitors enter the monastery on the third floor (it is built on a sloping site), where the separation of the outside world and the monastery is immediately made clear: the view into the inner court is broken by the concrete kiosks of the porter's lodge and the four parlatoria, the booths where visitors can speak to friars. Beyond this point lies the monastic life (La Tourette is now a study centre, the Centre Thomas More, and no longer a monastery). The 100 cells are arranged on the top two floors, distinguished from the exterior by the regular rectangular openings. The corridor for the cells runs around the courtyard, with only a thin slit at eye-level to allow views out. The floors below contain the

communal spaces, identified from the exterior by Le Corbusier's characteristic concrete lamellas arranged according to the Modulor. The only deviation from the basic U-shape is the protrusion of the pyramid-topped private chapel, the spiral staircases and the connecting corridors. Partly because of the minimal budget, but also because of Le Corbusier's sense of the austerity of the Dominicans, only a few of the walls are whitewashed and pipes and ducts, painted in what would today be called High-Tech colours, are everywhere exposed.

In contrast to the residential wing, which opens out to the surrounding woods, the church is a totally introverted, unadorned concrete box. The walls are left rough, and the light is low and carefully controlled: as at Ronchamp, there is a slit of light between walls and ceiling, and the ceiling itself has a single square panel of glass. Behind the friars' benches, horizontal slits with coloured glass provide filtered light for their books. The altar, in the middle of the church, is an island of white stone separating the friars from the lay congregation (who have their own access door) in the eastern half. The rectangular box of the sacristy adjoins the church to the south, and is lit by seven barrel-shaped roof-lights, each pointed at a different angle to catch the sun at different times of day. To the north of the main body of the church is the curved volume of the chapel of the Blessed Sacrament. The glow of the warm light from this chapel (also lit by the light barrels) suffuses throughout the church, so even the laymen, who are barred from the chapel, have a sense of the unseen mystery. □

architect
Le Corbusier

Youth centre 1960-5

| Next to stadium Firminy | 56 |

An industrial town near Saint-Etienne, Firminy, was badly damaged during the war. The mayor of Firminy, Claudius Petit, had commissioned Le Corbusier to build the Marseilles Unité ◇ 63 in his capacity as minister of reconstruction, so when he turned his attention to his own town, he naturally turned to Le Corbusier. The architect produced a grand scheme for the general redevelopment of the town, but when he died in 1965, the Unité was only partially complete and the youth centre was the only complete element. The church design, which derives from a sketch made by Le Corbusier in the twenties, was finalised just before his death but construction has stumbled on over two decades.

The youth centre was originally intended to overlook a proposed stadium, hence its unusual grandstand shape. When the

administration of Firminy decided to shift the stadium, Le Corbusier held to his original concept. The centre is entered from the east by an entrance ramp: the east façade is a regular grid of windows divided irregularly by concrete brise-soleil. The west façade, which was to have overlooked the stadium, is a sharply raked, rather blank wall of concrete pierced only by the single continuous line of windows. The concrete panel roof is supported on steel cables.
□

Villa Stein ('Les Terraces') 1926-7

| 17 rue du Prof. Pauchet Garches | 57 |

The Villa Stein, built for Gertrude Stein's brother, is one of the finest examples of Le Corbusier's 'five points of the new architecture', but it is far more refined than the slightly earlier Cook house ◇ 52. The Villa Stein's design is based on a system of proportion that prefigures Le Corbusier's famous Modulor, and has led the house to be compared to Palladio's Villa Foscari. Le Corbusier himself said about Villa Stein, 'In this case, mathematics provides some comforting truths: one leaves one's work with the certitude that the exact result has been reached.' The house has two distinct façades: the entrance façade is relatively closed, while large double-strip windows open up the garden façade. The ground floor, as always, contains the bare necessities of garage, entrance room, and (in this fairly grand house) servants' rooms. The first floor is the piano nobile, with living-room, dining-room, kitchen and enclosed terrace. The terrace, an open void chopped out of the garden façade (recalling Le Corbusier's 1925 L'Esprit Nouveau pavilion), is reached by a grand, sculptural stair from the garden. The stair stands completely free of the house, like a gangway to a great ocean liner. The upper two floors contain bedrooms and bathrooms, with the large roof terrace overlooking the garden.
□

Jean Renaudie

Centre Jeanne Hachette 1969-75

rue Lénine
Ivry-sur-Seine

58

Renaudie, who is responsible for a number of similar works in Ivry-sur-Seine, is perhaps the most extreme representative of those contemporary French architects obsessed with geometry. The Centre Jeanne Hachette, like his other works, is a maze built out of a complex series of acute triangles. The result is a sort of concrete-block garden of Babylon. The centre includes forty housing units, $6,500m^2$ of shops, $5,000m^2$ of offices, car parks and cinemas. The entire complex is built over a busy road.

☐

architect

Marcel Breuer

IBM research centre 1963

La Gaude

59

Breuer, who trained and later taught at the Bauhaus, is well known for his tubular steel Wassily chair, but in a long architectural career he married his industrial designer's eye for detail and proportion with an interest in the expression of structure. The IBM research centre is an elaboration on the UNESCO headquarters, Paris (1953-8), which Breuer designed in collaboration with Pier Luigi Nervi and Bernard Zehrfuss. The plan is a double-Y (or a curved-H), with the concrete structure carried on fair-face concrete pilotis. The use of pilotis suggest the influence of Le Corbusier, as does the deeply modelled façade (almost a brise-soleil), but Breuer's smoothness and symmetry sets him apart from Le Corbusier's work of the fifties and sixties.

☐

Hector Guimard

Coilliot house and shop 1898-1900

14 rue des Fleurs
Lille

60

The Coilliot house and shop, built for a family of ceramic manufacturers, is perhaps the most eccentric of Guimard's extant buildings. The narrow, irregular site led Guimard to create a balcony recess on the upper floors to regularise the planning. Eugène Gillet, who executed the signs for the Paris metro, made the yellow-green enamelled lava plaque on the façade. The upper floors, which contain the house, have a distinctly rustic image, with carved wood rather than stone on the exterior, compared with the ground floor shop. Although not all of the interior remains intact, the entrance hall consists of enamelled panels set in a cast-iron frame, the whole enlivened with Guimard's characteristically sinuous line.
☐

Vago and Freyssinet

Basilica of Saint Pius X 1956-8

Lourdes

61

Given a sensitive, unspoilt site, Vago and Freyssinet, one of the pioneering engineers of reinforced concrete, decided to construct a vast subterranean basilica. The flattened oval, 201 metres long, 81 metres wide and 11 metres high, can accommodate 20,000 persons. The twenty-nine elegant concrete portal frames support the thin slab roof and its top layer of turf. The cross members of the portal frames are carried on raked open triangular 'crutches': the cross members coincide with the radii of the great circles generating the plan. The central longitudinal ridge of the portal frames becomes a vast spine down the centre of the basilica, making the interior seem like a Modernist vision of the inside of Jonah's whale.
☐

Ricardo Bofill

Les Espaces d'Abraxas 1978-83

Noisy-le-grand
Marne-la-Vallée

62

France has been particularly unfortunate in its new towns: most of the post-war architecture is anonymous, poorly built and gimmicky. So the pre-cast concrete Classicism of Bofill is particularly extraordinary in France. But Bofill, and the successive governments who commission him, claim his architecture is merely a return to the great Classical traditions of French architecture. The complex of buildings at Noisy-le-Grand houses 600 flats in three major buildings: the eighteen-storey palace, the giant horseshoe of the theatre and the Arc de Triomphe-like arch. All construction is with concrete panels that are prefabricated off-site. Bofill's scale is enormous: giant order Doric columns house an eighteen-flight emergency stair. Bofill and his supporters claim this mail-order monumental Classicism is far more popular than typical modern housing, but the scale is so vast it is difficult to believe Bofill's housing projects will avoid the social problems that plague more conventional schemes.
□

280 boulevard Michelet
Marseilles

63

At the beginning of the fifties, two works of housing were completed that seemed a summation of architectural ideas and a spur to architects around the world. The first, finished in 1951, was Ludwig Mies van der Rohe's elegant steel and glass boxes on Lake Shore Drive in Chicago: this became the prototype for both housing, and more notably, office buildings throughout the world. The Unité d'habitation, Le Corbusier's massive unfinished-concrete block looming on the outskirts of Marseilles, was finished a year later. Le Corbusier intended the Unité as a prototype for the reconstruction of France: it proved too big, and too expensive, to serve such a sweeping role, but in other countries (Britain and Switzerland in particular) it was upheld as the banner of social housing. He did, however, build a number of other Unités in different cities ◇ 173, but none of them equalled the refinement of the Marseilles block.

The Unité is a vast reinforced concrete cage, containing 337 structurally independent housing units inserted like drawers in a desk. There are twenty-three variations of the housing unit, but most of them are split-level with a two-storey living-room at one end of the slab. Thus, internal corridors for access are only required every three floors: from each corridor, units can be entered on their upper level (on one side of the corridor) or their lower level (on the other side). In addition to the housing units, there are numerous 'community services', the most important being the shopping 'street' located halfway up the slab. From the exterior, this internal street is identified by the large screen of

pre-cast concrete brise-soleil. On the roof, a wonderland of Le Corbusier's sculptural genius with concrete, are playgrounds, a kindergarten, stage, crèche, swimming pool, running track and gymnasium.

The Unité, despite its enormous visual power, has significant problems as a model for housing. Le Corbusier, convinced of the validity of his Modulor (and also being rather short), left a height of only 2.26 metres in the single-height rooms. The inner rooms, which in some arrangements are childrens' bedrooms, are cupboard-like with no windows (sliding panels allow views through to other rooms). The internal street of shops has always been a commercial failure: both too large for the community and unattractive for retailers. The internal streets of the corridors are depressingly dark and gloomy (they run straight through the centre of the block for the entire 130 metres length). The ground floor, with its gargantuan pilotis supporting the seventeen upper storeys, is of intimidating scale. In fact, it is the scale of the Unité that creates the most misgivings today. The forms and ideas still seem heroic, when considered abstractly, but the Unité now seems like a vast, brilliantly accomplished architectural conceit. On the wide open plain outside Marseilles, the Unité dominates the landscape: there was no need here to build up. One Unité, however, is a treasure: fortunately Le Corbusier was never able to realise his ambition to build a series of Unités 200 or 300 metres apart in parkland, his Radiant City.

□

Theo van Doesburg

Van Doesburg house and studio 1929-31

29 rue Charles Infroit
Meudon

64

Van Doesburg, although not an architect, had profound influence on twentieth-century architecture through his leading role in the Dutch De Stijl movement. The greatest expression of De Stijl in architecture is Gerrit Rietveld's Schroeder house, Utrecht (1924) ◇ 276, but among the few buildings van Doesburg himself was responsible for, the studio and house he built for himself and his wife, Nelly, is interesting. Unlike the seemingly dynamic Schroeder house, with its horizontal and vertical planes bursting out of the cubic confines, the van Doesburg house is basically box-like. The influence of Le Corbusier, particularly his Citrohan projects of the early twenties, can be seen in the stilts, or <u>pilotis</u>, on which the house stands.
□

Prouvé and Sive

Houses 1950

83 route des Gardes
Meudon

65

After the war, Prouvé was involved in a number of designs of mass-produced houses to relieve the desperate housing shortage. The best of these projects, in Meudon, consisted of fourteen experimental houses using a variety of modern materials. A boxed metal floor, which contains the radiant heating, is placed upon a substructure of stone rubble. The lightweight steel portal-frame superstructure weighs less than 100 kilos, and is placed every four metres at right angles to the axis of the house. The roof truss consists of a ridge beam recessed into the portal frame, with two gable and two edge members. Aluminium panels are used for the roof cladding, while a false metal ceiling is used inside. The external panels are interchangeable and are recessed into the ribs of the frame. Windows and blinds retract into

the window breasts. At Meudon there are two versions of the house, one 8 x 8 metres, and the other 8 x 12 metres.
□

House 1901-2

| 22 rue de la Commanderie Nancy | **66** |

One of the heavier, more brooding works of the Nancy School, but notable for the extraordinary iron entrance gate which must have been influenced by Gaudi. Instead of the sinuous, flowing lines usually associated with art nouveau (and visible, to a degree, in the other ironwork of this house), the entrance gate is composed of large plates of iron, like a tropical jungle's massive foliage, heavily riveted together. Starbursts of abstract flowers burst out from the dense, almost intimidating, 'foliage'.

Villa Majorelle 1901-2

| 1 rue Louis Majorelle Nancy | **67** |

This early work of Sauvage, before his move to Paris and his pioneering housing designs, is one of the most wild and eccentric art nouveau houses of Nancy. The visual connection between art nouveau in Nancy and the grotesque of Gaudi in Barcelona can clearly be seen in the stalk-like chimneys that sprout from the roof. Sauvage's skill in composition, one of the strengths of his later work, is displayed in the plastic forms of the exterior: the art nouveau here is not a mere decorative style, but an impulse that infuses every part of the design. The interior has been very well preserved, and the most remarkable feature is the fireplace that looks like some great beast's yawning mouth. Louis Majorelle, the client, himself designed and made much of the furniture and the ironwork. Sauvage's collaborators, in fact, show how a provincial city like Nancy can witness one of the great flowerings of an architectural style, for the craftsmen that worked here are also responsible for most of the other fine houses of the period in Nancy: Jacques Grüber, for example, the glazier, also made the glass for Jacques-Réné Hermant on rue de Malzéville ◇ 70 and for Georges Biet and Eugène Vallin on rue de la Commanderie ◇ 66.

Emile André

Villa des Glycines 1902

5 rue des Brice Nancy	**68**

The Villa des Glycines is part of the art nouveau garden city conceived by André with Henri Gutton, of which unfortunately few buildings now remain. André's work has his signature ground-floor window: a low arched shape, outlined by radiating tiles. This window forms the mouth of what must be one of the most conscious 'buildings as faces' of the twentieth century. The first-floor bedroom windows form the eyes, the carved stone between expands downwards into the nose, and the arch of the ground-floor window becomes the great maw of some monster's mouth. The floral motifs usually associated with the art nouveau are more subtle here than in André's house on quai Claude-Le-Lorrain ◇ 69, but the ironwork of the first-floor balconies recalls some of Mackintosh's floral gates. The wistarias of the name (glycine) are vaguely echoed in the curvilinear shapes of the windows. ☐

architect

Emile André

House 1903

92·93 bis quai Lorrain Nancy	**69**

André's house on quai Claude-Le-Lorrain makes a good comparison with his contemporary Villa des Glycines ◇ 68. The same arch-shaped ground-floor window distinguishes the work, but here it looks more obviously floral: a giant tulip bud pushing its way up from the stem. The floral motif is carried through the decoration, particularly in the relief carving of the stone door surround and in the branch-like carving of the door itself. The entrance hall has particularly rich decoration. ☐

Jacques-Réné Hermant

House 1904

25 rue de Malzéville Nancy	**70**

Hermant's house is one of the more curious examples of the Nancy art nouveau, for from a distance it seems to be a typical eighteenth-century town-house. On closer examination, however, almost Gaudiesque details are revealed. The gate, for example, is a seemingly scribbled design of iron, recalling in a far more sober way the dragon gate of Gaudi's Finca Guell, Barcelona (1889). The entrance porch, which has been unfortunately modified behind its stone exterior, exhibits the brooding heaviness, almost grotesquerie, of the Nancy art nouveau that places it somewhere between typical French and Belgian works and the Germanic Jugendstil.

☐

architect

Gutton and Hornecker

Villa Marguerite 1905

3 rue du Colonel-Rénard Nancy	**71**

Part of the garden city planned by Emile André and Gutton, the Villa Marguerite is among the more eccentric survivors of the original scheme. The roughly hewn stone and its eclectic outline link it to the rustic art nouveau style defined by Hector Guimard's now-demolished Castel Henriette, Sèvres (1899-1900). Among the more unusual features of the Villa Marguerite are the belvedere, which has been modified over the years, and the large knife-shaped window that lights the main staircase to the right of the entrance porch.

☐

architect
Roland Simounet

Musée de la Préhistoire d'Ile de France 1974-9

Route de Sens (Rd 225)
Nemours **72**

Simounet is well known for his work on new towns in Algeria, notably the simple concrete and brick community at Timgad (1959-62). His work there was inspired by the low budget, the lack of skilled labour, the scarcity of materials, but much of the primitive aesthetic he developed in Algeria carries over to his work in France. Simounet's museum in Nemours is a simple structure of rough concrete which seems to grow out of its site: the vertical forms of concrete echo the trees, the base reflects the boulder-strewn landscape. The exhibition rooms are linked by glazed galleries and separated by the internal garden courts.
☐

architect
Michel Roux-Spitz

Housing 1929-31

45 boulevard d'Inkermann
Neuilly-sur-Seine **73**

If Roux-Spitz's works today seem unremarkable, it is because his style, the archetypal <u>Moderne</u>, was vastly influential, imitated widely in France, Britain and the United States. Roux-Spitz created a successful twentieth-century version of the bourgeois town house: Classically symmetrical, clad in stone, with central bow windows for the main living-room. He also created an interior style to match the elegant façades. Reception rooms were luxurious and comfortable, with marble-clad walls and mirrors to visually increase the size. The private rooms continued this theme of expensive materials, but with less ostentation. Roux-Spitz said that the servant spaces (kitchen, laundry, etc.) should resemble a clinic. The housing on boulevard d'Inkermann is one of his best and most typical works: other characteristic signs of his work are the penthouse duplex and the decorative metal on the roofline.
☐

architect

Le Corbusier

Jaoul house 1952-4

81 rue de Longchamp
Neuilly-sur-Seine | **74**

The Jaoul houses (a pair built for the parents and for the son and his wife) are an extension of the ideas Le Corbusier first developed in the weekend house in St Cloud (1935). The three-storeyed Jaoul houses are designed around a sequence of parallel naves of different lengths: these are defined by the low concrete 'Catalan' vaults. Rough finished brickwork is used both inside and outside, something Le Corbusier first experimented with in his penthouse on rue Nungésser-et-Coli. The vaults themselves are finished with tiles. The structure, clearly expressed by the exposed materials, is of brick walls supporting the concrete beams and vaults. It was this rough, undisguised use of materials that was so influential, especially with the British Brutalists. In planning, the

Jaoul houses are not as adventurous as Le Corbusier's early houses, with their free plans. Instead, the Jaoul houses have simple, basically rectilinear plans, for Le Corbusier hoped to recapture what he saw as the simplicity of Mediterranean seaside living in these suburban works. Placed at right angles to one another, the houses share an entrance and service court.

☐

architect

Frantz Jourdain

Samaritaine department store 1891-1907

rue de la Monnaie
Paris 1 | **75**

The modern department store originated in Paris, with Boileau and Eiffel's 1876 Bon Marché, but its best art nouveau incarnation was in La Samaritaine. Jourdain converted twenty-three old houses into the single commercial structure organised around internal courts. The iron frame is straightforwardly expressed, but it is encrusted with typical floral decoration. The large windows are framed by a series of polychromatic faience panels, sadly now covered: these panels bore characteristic art nouveau decoration as well as publicity for the products inside the store. Henri Sauvage extensively modified La Samaritaine in 1926.

☐

Saint-Jean de Montmartre 1894-1904

10 rue des Abbesses
Paris 18

76

De Baudot is an interesting figure who spans several generations of French architecture. His studies began in the studio of Henri Labrouste, designer of the great Bibliothèque Sainte-Geneviève (1843-50), but in 1856 he moved to join Eugène Emmanuel Viollet-le-Duc, the titanic French medievalist. De Baudot proved the most capable and enduring of Viollet-le-Duc's disciples: Saint-Jean de Montmartre was started fifteen years after the master's death. Saint-Jean is, therefore, a bridge between the giants of the nineteenth century and the new architecture of the twentieth. The reinforced concrete of the vaguely Gothic structure of the church raises immediate comparisons with the work of Auguste Perret, who, by the time de Baudot's church was completed, had far surpassed the older architect in structural invention. But de Baudot's work was enormously innovatory: the concrete frame is plainly exposed on the exterior, contrasting with the non-load-bearing brick walls. Inside, as with the great Gothic cathedrals, the structure is the principal decoration. Faïence mosaics are used to decorate the concrete structural members. ☐

Castel Béranger 1894-9

14-16 rue La Fontaine
Paris 16

77

In 1894, the Salon des Artistes Françaises awarded Guimard a travel grant to further his design education. His travels took him to Brussels where, encountering the nascent art nouveau of Victor Horta, Guimard's own future style was determined. Upon his return to Paris, he embarked on the design of the building that became his masterpiece, the Castel Béranger. The six-storey, thirty-eight-unit apartment block has an eclectic façade of rubble stone, coloured brick, millstone, sandstone and glazed ceramic tile. The cast-iron balcony ornaments writhe with even more vigour than the contemporary work in Brussels. Guimard's detractors, unsurprisingly, called it the Castel déranger.
Guimard's decoration and planning are equally remarkable. The extraordinary abstract entrance gate, made of wrought iron and copper, was executed by the artist, Balet, following a drawing of Guimard's. The courtyard fountain is almost Expressionist in its liquid, flowing form. The ceramic panels that decorate the entrance hall reject the naturalistic decoration of Horta and his followers for something far more mysterious. The Castel Béranger is planned along two axes, one running through the entrances and staircases of the front and rear blocks, the other at right angles through the courtyard.
The building is thus divided into two equal halves with three flats per floor on each side. Main and service staircases are placed back to back. ☐

Apartment building 1902-3

25 bis rue Franklin
Paris 16

79

Perret's apartment building on rue Franklin marks one of the first effective uses of reinforced concrete in architecture. In keeping with the dominant Parisian style of the day, rue Franklin is influenced by art nouveau. But it is Perret's structure and planning, rather than his decoration, that is of most interest. The rigidly symmetrical building has a clearly visible structural framework of straight vertical and horizontal members: unlike Chédanne's contemporary Parisien Libéré offices ◇ 80, Perret's basic forms are uninfluenced by the art nouveau. Glazed tiles clad the concrete giving the work, in the sunlight, an extraordinary iridescence. Windows are invariably framed by projecting bands of plain tiles. The planning is designed to allow a maximum of natural light into the apartments. Rooms are grouped around the small court carved out of the front of the building: the three principal rooms on each floor, the dining-room, drawing-room and bedroom, are the three central bays and open into one another. The elaborate stoneware floral decoration on the façade is by Alexandre Bigot.
◻

architect
Hector Guimard

Porte Dauphine metro station 1898-1901

avenue Foch
Paris 16

78

In 1896 the Compagnie du Metropolitain launched a competition for the design of the entrances to their new stations. Guimard did not enter the competition, but the president, Adrien Benard, an admirer of art nouveau, awarded the commission to him anyway. Guimard designed three basic types of entrance: open steps with railings (of which many still survive), enclosed and covered steps (only Porte Dauphine survives), and complete pavilions (none survive). Although Guimard's designs feature exuberant floral decoration, with the scale of the commission in mind, all of the cast-iron work is modular panels, pre-cast and easily interchanged or replaced. Porte Dauphine has an iron frame with enamelled panels decorated with a sinuous pattern, and

translucent wired glass. A central girder, which incorporates a rainwater gutter, supports a butterfly-shaped glass roof.
◻

Le Parisien Libéré offices 1903-4

124 rue Réaumur
Paris 2

80

Chédanne, who trained at the Ecole des Beaux-Arts, was, like many architects of his generation, influenced by art nouveau. In his masterpiece, however, he transforms the masonry-based aesthetic of art nouveau into one of the most elegant iron structures of any age. The Parisien Libéré office, on one of Paris' grand Haussmann boulevards, has five storeys of iron and glass topped by a sixth storey and attic of brick. The flowing lines of Chédanne's iron structure refer clearly to the prevalent art nouveau decoration of the time, but here the decorative urge is subordinate to the structural necessities. The three large bay windows of the fourth floor, for example, are supported on elegantly curved iron consoles which form an ideal structure for the ribbed brick vaults under the bays. The floral root of Chédanne's shapes can be best seen on the ground floor, where the iron ribs curve symmetrically in like some abstracted tree's branches. The iron gates of the entrance, although with comparatively stripped decoration, are far more typical of the art nouveau architecture of the time. With his iron structure, and his formalised art nouveau, Chédanne's design seems thoroughly modern in its high proportion of window to structure.

☐

Housing 1908-11

17-21 rue La Fontaine
Paris 16

81

Guimard's late housing on rue La Fontaine, near his early master-piece, the Castel Béranger ◇ 77 is the best of his later art nouveau works. The exuberant, in some eyes outrageous, eclecticism of his early works has given way to a more refined, restrained decorative style, akin to the style of Horta's Hallet house ◇ 10. The most characteristic exterior flourish is the first-floor window's stone mullion cascading over the entrance.

☐

Housing 1912

26 rue Vavin
Paris 6

82

Sauvage's first low-cost housing block, on rue Vavin, set a pattern for many of his later designs. Given the strict Paris regulations about cornice-line and ridge-line, Sauvage stepped his building back to give a terrace and light to the apartments. The first two floors are level with the other buildings on the street, but each of the five floors above step back. Most significantly, Sauvage clad his building with glazed white and blue bricks in a decorative manner: this has ensured the work's almost spotless condition over many years. One of Sauvage's best details is the way the glazed bricks gently curve into the terrace parapets. At the time of his work on rue Vavin, Sauvage was still inexperienced in many technical aspects of building: after his initial application for a building permit was rejected, the masonry walls at ground level had to be thickened enormously to provide adequate support.

Ozenfant house 1922-3

53 avenue Reille
Paris 14

83

Le Corbusier built the small house on avenue Reille, one of his first Paris commissions, for his friend and colleague Amédée Ozenfant. The house is basically a simple box, with the top-floor study lit by the large windows on the north and east façades. Saw-tooth roof-lights, now sadly removed, provided a filter of natural light from above. Le Corbusier's attempt to 'liberate' buildings from the ground can be seen in its embryonic stage here: the main entrance is at the top of the external spiral stair (which in itself became a continuing motif) on the first floor, with the ground floor devoted to the garage (now converted into a room).

Housing 1922

13 rue des Amiraux
Paris 18

84

Sauvage's low-cost apartment building on rue des Amiraux extends the vocabulary he started on rue Vavin in 1912 ◇ 82: terraces progressively stepping back, glazed brick, conventional construction. But rue des Amiraux is a far larger, more ambitious work. The basically symmetrical design steps back from two streets, with flats arranged around a central internal courtyard. On the lower floors, the courtyard contains a covered swimming pool, where Sauvage's inventive, decorative use of glazed brick reaches its zenith. The pool has recently been magnificently restored by the City of Paris. Despite the formal similarities with rue Vavin, Sauvage here turns away from the curving lines of his earlier work, and revels in the juxtaposition of hard-edged brick shapes. Only at the corners overlooking the terraces and in the dividing walls on the terraces themselves does Sauvage's earlier line return.

□

La Roche and Jeanneret houses 1923

Sq. de Docteur Blanche
Paris 16

85

The two adjoining houses at the end of a small, tree-lined street now house the Fondation Le Corbusier, and at the time of their completion they were the architect's most advanced and adventurous design. The Jeanneret house is fairly typical of Le Corbusier's work of the time, but the L-shaped La Roche house marks a number of departures. The three-storeyed entrance hall is the focal point of the design, with walkways, stairs, rooms cutting into the soaring space. A bulging gallery, which seems from the outside to be pushing its way up the street, forms the other half of the L. The three strips of windows at the top of the bowed wall filter north light into the gallery, which originally housed Raoul La Roche's collection of Cubist paintings. The gallery is reached by a ramp from the second-floor library (which itself overlooks the entrance hall). Ramps, following this gallery ramp, became a continuing motif in Le Corbusier's designs, culminating in the large central ramp of the Carpenter Center for the Visual Arts (1961-4) at Harvard University.

□

Adolf Loos

Tristan Tzara house 1926-7

15 avenue Junot
Paris 18

86

The Viennese architect is best known for his 1908 essay 'Ornament and Crime' (Le Corbusier later called it a 'Homeric cleansing' of architecture). But the stern, completely unadorned exteriors of Loos' works often hide a surprisingly decorative interior. Loos settled in Paris in 1922, and his house there for the Dadaist Tzara is one of his finest late works. A tall, blank façade, slightly concave in plan, has a two-storey void sunk into the centre. The interior has an open plan, with the dining-room opening into the living-room, but on a higher level.
☐

Henri Sauvage

Housing 1926

65 rue La Fontaine
Paris 16

87

Sauvage's low-cost apartments on rue La Fontaine mark his change from the stepped terraces of the 1912 rue Vavin and the 1922 rue des Amiraux housing. He retains the characteristic glazed brick, here white, yellow and blue, but uses over-scaled bay windows as his new device for natural light. The bay windows, at the corners and the middles of the façades, were for double-height artists' studios. These strangely proportioned bays, allied with the rather quirky decorative pattern of glazed bricks, animate the otherwise conventional block of housing.
☐

Planeix house 1927

24 bis boulevard Massena
Paris 13

88

The Planeix house, like the contemporary Villa Stein at Garches ◇ 57, is a symmetrically composed house illustrating Le Corbusier's famous five points of the new architecture.

The two most interesting aspects of the Planeix house, one of the less well known of Le Corbusier's designs, are the projecting living-room on the first floor which emphasises the central axis of the house, and the open concrete staircase on the garden. The ground floor has two studio apartments to the left and right of the central garage (the ground floor as the zone of motion), each 4.5 metres high with a gallery running at midpoint around the side with room for a bed, small kitchen, bathroom and cupboard. The top floor has a much larger studio lit by roof-lights.

□

Netherlands students' hostel 1927-8

Cité Universitaire
Paris 13

89

In 1926, the City of Paris began the Cité Universitaire, a vast area near the Porte d'Orléans where foreign students could live in national hostels. The buildings are today virtually an exhibition of twenties and thirties architecture, but, with three exceptions, they are fairly undistinguished. Le Corbusier's two contributions, the Swiss pavilion (1930-2) ◇ 94 and the Brazilian pavilion (1956-9) ◇ 97, are well known, but Dudok's Dutch pavilion is less familiar. Although not reaching the heights of his town hall, Hilversum (1928-30) ◇ 273, the Dutch pavilion is a good illustration of how Dudok adapted the aesthetics of De Stijl to his own modern idiom. The hostel is built up from blocky, rectilinear components, with only the stair-tower exhibiting any curve. The windows along boulevard Jourdan are in horizontal strips, but those facing the inner court and garden are in more traditional groupings.

□

Robert Mallet-Stevens

Houses 1927

Chareau and Bijvoet

Dalsace house (Maison de Verre) 1928-31

rue Mallet-Stevens Paris 16	90

Mallet-Stevens was one of the key figures in the development of Modern, rational architecture, but, perhaps because of the overwhelming dominance of Le Corbusier in France, is not very well known today. His work combined a variety of influences, but in his five houses and a caretaker's lodge on the eponymous street the clearest precedents are the Dutch movement De Stijl and the art deco. Rue Mallet-Stevens was the architect's idea: he convinced four clients (the fifth house was his own) to purchase adjacent sites so that he could create a homogenous scheme. All of the houses are composed of simple rectilinear shapes, with the exception of the grand circular stair-tower of the best-preserved house, No. 11. The four-storey No. 11, built for the sculptors Joel and Jan Martel, is built around the cylindrical tower: the ground floor was the sculptors' studio, with living quarters above. Numerous artists collaborated with Mallet-Stevens on the houses: Barillet for the decorative glass, Prouvet for the elaborate main doors and Gabriel Guevrekian for some of the interiors.
☐

31 rue Saint-Guillaume Paris 7	91

Dr Jean Dalsace and his wife Anna gave Chareau and Bijvoet the commission to design a house that would fit into the first three floors of an eighteenth-century building in 1928. The architects took this as an opportunity to create one of the truly remarkable houses of the twentieth century. The Maison de Verre is in some senses the realisation of the dream of the Expressionists of a pure glass architecture, but in its meticulous details and planning it becomes something far different from the visions of a decade earlier. In today's terminology, the Maison de Verre is the first great High-Tech building. The walls of St Gobain glass-lens block are held together in an undisguised steel frame. The window-wall conceals at first-floor level the double-height living-room: Pirelli rubber tiles are used for flooring, the bookshelves are of tubular metal, the steel I-beams and their rivets soar proudly exposed in the space. Most of the furniture is by Chareau with fabrics by André Lurçat. This is the house's most extraordinary room (the doctor's surgery is on the ground floor), but the same innovative use of materials and attention to details is present throughout the house. The master bathroom, for example, has cabinetry made from duralumin, a corrosion-resistant alloy of aluminium. The shelf is of brass.
☐

Salvation Army hostel (Cité de Refuge) 1929-33

12 rue Cantagrel
Paris 13

92

The Cité de Refuge, now badly altered, was the first of Le Corbusier's buildings, and one of the first in the world to be hermetically sealed for air-conditioning. Forced air provided the ventilation, but the massive wall of glass on the south façade created far too much heat gain inside and after the war Pierre Jeanneret replaced the glass wall with opening windows set in a concrete frame. The basic form of Le Corbusier's work remains, however: the social services wing is an autonomous volume, clearly distinct from the slab of the refuge itself. Visitors enter at the box-shaped porter's lodge, from where they are propelled over a foot-bridge into the circular lobby where they are received by the 'social officer'.

☐

Housing 1929-34

3-5 boulevard Victor
Paris 15

93

Patout is widely known for the interior design of the ocean liners L'Atlantique (1928, with Emile-Jacques Ruhlmann) and Normandie (1934), so it is entirely appropriate that his best building resembles a giant ocean liner run aground in the middle of Paris. Patout acquired the thin, wedge-shaped site in 1929: over 90 metres long, its width runs from 2.4 metres to only 10 metres. Patout's solution, undoubtedly conditioned by his naval work, is an unadorned, great white wedge of housing. His own apartment, a triplex with a large balcony, forms the prow. The ground floor is composed of shops, while above, on the first and second floors, duplex apartments have the only vertical apertures in the entire building. The three floors above these consist of rows of apart-ments whose horizontal windows resemble the decks of an ocean liner. The top two floors are again duplex apartments, arranged in regular blocks – perhaps the five smoke-stacks of this landlocked liner.

☐

Pavillon Suisse 1930-2

Cité Universitaire
Paris 13

94

The Pavillon Suisse, a student hostel for Swiss students in Paris, is the first of Le Corbusier's 'slab' buildings and was labelled by him as 'a veritable laboratory of modern architecture'. The rectangular main block of housing is a steel-framed slab standing on six large reinforced concrete pilotis. These pilotis stand in contrast to the spindly columns of Le Corbusier's houses at the time, and mark an intermediate step in his progression to the truly massive pilotis of the Marseilles Unité ◇ 63 . Adjoining this simple slab, which is 'liberated from the soil', to use Le Corbusier's phrase, is an irregularly shaped block containing the stairwell and ground-floor communal spaces. In contrast to the slab, the adjoining block seems to grow out of the ground.

The large curved wall of the common-room became the focus for a dispute during the design. Against Le Corbusier's wishes, pictures of mountain scenery were tried out on the wall, but the curve proved too difficult a surface on which to hang pictures successfully. Le Corbusier came up with the idea of a photo-mural, something that had not been done before. The first photo-mural used enlarged photographs of micro-organisms and crystals, but this was considered scandalous and was replaced. During the war, the Nazis, who used the roof of the Pavillon Suisse for their anti-aircraft guns, removed the second photo-mural. Justice was finally done after the war when Le Corbusier was commissioned to produce a mural.

☐

Apartments 1933

24 rue Nungésser-et-Coli
Paris 16

95

This eight-storey apartment building is primarily of interest because Le Corbusier built the top two floors as his own penthouse, in which he lived until his death in 1965. The street façade is a very Classical composition, using glass blocks to define the lower level of each floor. In his own apartment, Le Corbusier left the stone party-wall exposed as a contrast to his own smooth plaster surfaces, perhaps an example of incipient Brutalism.

☐

<table>
<tr><td>architect</td></tr>
<tr><td>Jean Ginsberg</td></tr>
</table>

Housing 1934

42 avenue de Versailles Paris 16	**96**

Ginsberg worked for a few months with Le Corbusier and then with André Lurçat, two of the principal forces behind French Modern architecture, but his personal style adds overtones of the art deco or Moderne style. Ginsberg's 1934 building on avenue de Versailles is one of the finer corner buildings of the early Moderns: the quarter-circle of the corner acts as a visual hinge for the two halves of the block and sweeps the eye around. Ginsberg borrows his motifs from a variety of sources. The strip-window corner seems almost German, the rather nautical balconies are from early Le Corbusier, and the plastic forms of the skyline are variations on Le Corbusier's Villa Savoye roof ◇ 100.
☐

<table>
<tr><td>architect</td></tr>
<tr><td>Le Corbusier</td></tr>
</table>

Brazilian students' hostel 1956-9

Cité Universitaire Paris 13	**97**

The Brazilian students' hostel makes an interesting comparison with the nearby Pavillon Suisse ◇ 94 , designed twenty-five years apart. The form is roughly similar: the slab of housing supported on pilotis rising above the distinct communal buildings. But where Le Corbusier contrasted the smooth slab and the rough low block in the earlier design, now all the materials are rough and crude. The slab is of rough-finished concrete as is the single-storeyed administration block. The wedge-shaped commonroom further recalls the Pavillon Suisse with its similar rubble walls.
☐

Communist Party headquarters 1968-71

place du Colonel-Fabien
Paris 10

98

Niemeyer, Brazil's best-known architect, started his career by collaborating with Le Corbusier on the Ministry of Education and Health building in Rio de Janeiro (1936-45). His personal style, profoundly influenced by his association with Le Corbusier, also includes free-style elements more closely linked to Brazilian Baroque. The Communist Party head-quarters is a smooth, double-curved glass box built on a concrete hill. The domed roof of the underground auditorium emerges out of this concrete base. Niemeyer's own leather and steel furniture is used inside. The glass box of offices has an immaculately detailed curtain wall.

The Centre Pompidou, popularly known as Beaubourg, is one of the few buildings that splits all viewers pro and con. No one is neutral, least of all Parisians, about the enormous cultural centre with its structure and services exposed like an oil refinery or Meccano creation. The very incongruity, the surprise, of Beaubourg in the midst of the beautiful uniformity of Paris is what makes it one of the most contentious buildings of the twentieth century. Beaubourg hides in the fabric of Paris, so when a corner in Le Marais is turned, revealing an enormous structural member, or when an axis of streets suddenly opens up to a view of the varied, brightly coloured roofscape, the surprise and, for some, delight, is startling. Piano and Rogers' Beaubourg resulted from a major international competition in 1970. The original design called for an extremely flexible building, with an exterior alive with megagraphic displays and internal mezzanines that could be shifted according to varying needs. The mezzanines were fixed when costs began to escalate (though Beaubourg was actually completed on time and on budget) and the megagraphics have fortunately given way to the carefully articulated external structure and services. The concept of Beaubourg can be traced back in the twentieth century with notable precursors such as Jean Prouvé's 1938-9 Maison du Peuple market at Clichy ◇ 54 and the work of the Archigram group in London in the 1960s. Archigram advocated flexible, movable, demountable buildings and, in their drawings and collages, made graphics and pop imagery an important part of their design.

But Pompidou stands as a strikingly original work that managed to realise what had for the most part been architectural dreams. The quality of Pompidou rests to a large extent on the structural engineering by Peter Rice of Ove Arup and Partners, as the appearance relies on the proportions of the structural details, the clarity and coherence of their design, much as the beauty of a Gothic cathedral is created by its decorative, yet functional structure. In a massive building, the profusion of structural elements helps break down the scale and humanise the work.

For the Pompidou is truly massive: in the 100,000m² there are the national museum of modern art, a major reference library, a centre of industrial design, a centre for music and acoustic research (which is underground), and supporting services such as car park, restaurant, etc. The extraordinary popular success of all this has, of course, created problems. Five times as many persons use the centre as were originally estimated, resulting in enormous wear and tear on the building. The interior is disappointing, particularly with the crowds, after the spectacle of the exterior. But the extraordinary exterior makes these criticisms quibbles. With fire-eaters, jugglers and mime artists crowding the plaza modelled on Siena's Campo (the Brancusi studio which stifles one end was a government-imposed late addition) Beaubourg is one of Paris' most lively areas. The building has been responsible for the revitalisation of a large area of Paris. Beaubourg's impact is unique and so the building should remain unique: a Paris filled with Beaubourgs is a horrifying thought.

□

Centre Georges Pompidou 1970-7

place du Georges Pompidou
Paris 4

99

Villa Savoye ('Les heures claires') 1928-31

82 chemin de Villiers
Poissy

100

The Villa Savoye, probably the most famous of Le Corbusier's houses, originally sat in the midst of a great field with expansive views out of the continuous strip windows of the first floor. Now, unfortunately, the views and the field are marred by the inappropriately named Ecole Le Corbusier next door. But the history of the Villa Savoye is not entirely sad, for it was saved from virtual ruin in 1967 by the French government and its Cultural Minister, André Malraux. Following the restoration, the Villa Savoye can be seen again as a pristine, white box, standing on its twenty-six slender pilotis. The plan is of a perfect square, but the ground floor only contains a thumb-shaped area containing servants' quarters and a garage for three cars. Le Corbusier defined the ground as the 'zone of motion', and here is his best example of this definition, for the car reigns supreme: the radius of the arc of the ground floor was determined by the minimum turning radius of the owner's car. The first floor is reached either by the stunningly elegant curved concrete staircase, or by the gently sloping ramp. Both stair and ramp climb through all three levels, creating a counterpoint between the two and emphasising vertical motion and vistas. The first floor contains the main rooms of the house: the long living-room along one wall with views down the Seine valley, the three bedrooms and bathrooms. These rooms are grouped around the first-floor terrace, visibly contained within the volume of the house by the framing screens.

architect

François Spoerry

Port Grimaud 1966-81

Route Nationale 98

101

Port Grimaud, a resort village for the wealthy on the Riviera, is commercially and architecturally the brainchild of Spoerry. He rejected the typically debased Modernism that passed for architecture in the south of France, and decided to create a village that would mimic the forms of the spontaneous, vernacular Mediterranean towns taking inspiration in part from Clough William-Ellis' Portmeirion ◇ 249. The result resembles somewhat a Walt Disney-view of Mediterranean vernacular, but its success has made it one of the touchstones for those architects who reject Modernism and look to traditional forms for their inspiration. The logic behind Spoerry's plan was to provide every house with a mooring for a yacht (a keen yachtsman himself, he knew the luxury this would represent). So Port Grimaud is a planned Venice, with canals snaking their way in and out of the fingers of land with terraces of picturesquely designed houses. The construction of the foundations for the peninsulas and of the houses themselves is concrete. The very success of Port Grimaud has led to a slight watering down of the concept in the later stages, where the idea of a mooring outside everyone's back door has been abandoned to fit in more units in less space.

□

architect

Zehrfuss and Prouvé

Palais du CNIT 1955-9

place de La Défense
Puteaux-La-Défense

102

The giant exhibition hall at La Défense is more an engineering feat than architecture: the double self-supporting reinforced concrete shell covers a vast equilateral triangle with sides 238 metres long. The shell is made up of triangular wedges tied together to form three fans spreading from the abutments. Under this one roof is 105,000m^2 of exhibition space. The three large glass walls were detailed by the engineer Jean Prouvé.

□

Fleetguard factory 1981

Route Nationale 165
Quimper

103

It is no surprise that locals in Quimper have dubbed the Fleetguard factory l'araignée (the spider) and le chapiteau (the circus), for the tall steel masts of the structure, with their cables in tension, do resemble some strange creature or a futuristic circus tent. With engineer Peter Rice, Richard Rogers & Partners designed a simple box based entirely around the notion of a suspended structure. The steel masts are arranged in an 18-metre grid, and through an elegantly detailed array of tension rods the simple, steel-clad factory shed is supported. Fleetguard makes an interesting comparison with another Rogers work, the Inmos factory, Newport, Wales ◇ 243, which is far more complex in its suspended structure, and with Foster Associates' Renault warehouse, Swindon, England ◇ 253, which shares some of the simplicity of Fleetguard. Fleetguard, however, is the more stripped-down of the structures: a problem reduced to its essentials. ☐

Notre Dame church 1923-4

avenue de la Résistance
Raincy

104

Perret was one of the great pioneers in the use of reinforced concrete, notably in his apartment building on rue Franklin in Paris (1902-3) ◇ 79 , but his most radical use came in the church of Notre Dame. Intended as a memorial for the fallen at the battle of Ourcq, the budget for the church was extremely low. Perret seized the opportunity to explore the monumental qualities of unadorned reinforced concrete. The church is basilical in plan, with aisles and an apse, but Perret's accomplishment was to achieve, as the Gothic master builders had attempted centuries before, an enclosure almost entirely of glass with minimal supporting elements. The concrete, everywhere left bare, is reduced to the minimum, particularly in the reed-like free-standing columns. These columns, which are — visually — almost disturbingly thin, support the segmental shell vault of the nave and smaller crosswise vaults over the aisles. The walls are of pre-cast concrete units, with coloured glass designs by Maurice Denis in regular patterns. Outside, the concrete and glass box is rather stern, but the stepped spire, composed of standard reinforced concrete elements, has a distinctly Gothic outline. ☐

Le Corbusier's pilgrimage chapel at Ronchamp is one of the icons of the twentieth century. The curving, free forms of this extraordinary object, standing on the hill overlooking the village and the plain of the Saône, mark Le Corbusier's distinct break with the architecture of his early years to create something organic and primitive rather than mechanistic and modern. He accepted the commission for the chapel in 1950, although he was at first reluctant, having been disappointed in his 1948 scheme for a retreat at La Sainte-Beaume after the veto of the French ecclesiastic authorities. But at the time of the chapel's consecration in 1955, Le Corbusier wrote to the archbishop of Besançon, 'In building this chapel, I wished to create a place of silence, of prayer, of peace, of spiritual joy. A sense of what was sacred inspired our efforts. Some things are sacred, others are not — whether they be outwardly religious or otherwise.... It was a project difficult, meticulous, primitive, made strong by the resources brought into play but sensitive and informed by all-embracing mathematics which is the creator of that space which cannot be described in words.' The small chapel, which can hold a congregation of only 200, is defined by three massive walls and the sweeping, shell-shaped concrete roof. The walls are partially built up from Vosges stone, taken from the rubble of the old chapel destroyed in the war, but they are mostly a framing of steel reinforcing bars covered with a mesh that was sprayed with concrete and painted white. Enormously thick, in places up to 3 metres, the walls themselves contain the three tiny side-chapels. The great overhanging roof rests on thin reinforced concrete columns, set almost invisibly in the thickness of the wall. Hence there

is a 15-centimetre gap all round between the roof and wall, creating a delicate filtering of light that seems to lift the roof up without support (the roof itself is actually constructed of two thin membranes of reinforced concrete, covered on top by aluminium sheathing). Le Corbusier's handling of light both inside and outside the chapel is perhaps the most extraordinary aspect of the design. The thick south wall is pierced with dozens of rectangular holes, creating deep embrasures and windows of clear, painted and coloured glass. The effect inside is of softly filtered, coloured light. The side-chapels are lit from the towers above: two of the side-chapels are painted brilliant red and purple, virtually the only deviation from the clean white that prevails in the design.

The dynamic shape of the chapel, and the sculptural qualities of the punctures and extrusions from its surface, form the backdrop for the outdoor congregations that gather at Ronchamp. For, at Notre-Dame-du-Haut, Le Corbusier was in a sense reclaiming the dramatic role of architecture. The east end houses an external altar and pulpit, sheltering underneath the huge eave of the roof. Although Le Corbusier himself said that Ronchamp is a 'space which cannot be described in words', he offered the best advice on how to see it: 'Observe the play of shadows, learn the game . . . Precise shadows, precisely delineated, but with what enchanting arabesques and frets. Counterpoint and fugue. Great music. Try to look at the picture upside-down. You will soon discover the game.' □

Henri-Edouard Ciriani

La Cour d'Angle housing 1978-82

26 rue Auguste-Poullain
Saint-Denis

106

Ciriani is one of the few French architects of the seventies and eighties who has continued to work in a distinctly Modern idiom with confidence. His Saint-Denis housing, although complex and decorative, relies almost totally on the expression of its structure for effect. The monumentalism of the work is partly a response to what Ciriani saw as the complete disorder of the surrounding buildings. His design emphasises the depth of the building: structural screens are pierced with large square openings, walls are regularly broken through with balconies, terraces or windows.
□

architect

Paul Chemetov

Skating rink 1973-80

rue du Docteur-Bauer
Saint-Ouen

107

Chemetov's skating rink, on an island site cleared for proposed road work which never materialised, derives from the unrealised projects of the Russian Constructivists of the twenties. A cantilevered deck lifted clear of the roads contains the skating rink; the ground floor is used for car parking. Two pairs of steel towers support the vast main beams from which the building is suspended and clearly define the vertical circulation to the skating rink.
□

architect

José-Luis Sert

Fondation Maeght 1964

Saint-Paul-de-Vence | **108**

Sert, born and trained in Barcelona, started his architectural career working with Le Corbusier. The influence is clear in his work, but as the Fondation Maeght shows, Sert developed a far more intimate, perhaps delicate style. The concrete structure bears a striking resemblance to parts of Le Corbusier's work at Chandigarh (1950-8), especially the curved concrete canopies on the roof. But where the surfaces of Chandigarh are rough, Sert's surfaces are always smooth. The plan is village-like, with buildings informally grouped around courtyards at different levels. The complex consists of a public area with exhibition halls, a cinema, library, bookshop and cafeteria, and a private study centre for artists.

☐

architect

Ricardo Bofill

Les Arcades du Lac housing 1972-8

Montigny-le-Bretonneux
Saint-Quentin-en-Yvelines | **109**

Les Arcades du Lac was the first realisation of Bofill's prefabricated, concrete Classicism. The Palacio d'Abraxas, Marne-la-Vallée (1978-83) ◇ 62, is a far grander conception, but the earlier project contains the main concepts: axial, Beaux-Arts planning, stripped Classical detailing, what Bofill calls 'Versailles for the people'. But the confident, at times intimidating, scale and bravura of the later project are lacking in Les Arcades du Lac. The buildings are a little too puny to sustain their applied Classical grandeur, and the details are far too crude. But Bofill's work must be judged in comparison with the often execrable housing that surrounds it in these Paris new towns.

☐

Cité artisanale des Bruyères 1963-5, 1978

5 rue Carle-Vernet
Sèvres

110

Georges Candilis, who was Le Corbusier's site architect for the Marseilles Unité ◇ 63 , established his practice with the Yugoslav Alexis Josic and the American Shadrach Woods in the mid-fifties. Their work, based on rational, geometric structural systems was immensely influential in the sixties in Europe. But their large schemes, such as the Free University of Berlin (1963), no longer create the excitement that they once did. Smaller works, however, such as the collection of workshops in Sèvres, remain interesting examples of sixties rationalism. The 5,000m² of workshops and offices (another 1,700m² was added in 1978) are constructed with a concrete frame with a module of 4.5 metres. The frame is filled in with concrete panels or windows as required. All of the interior spaces receive ample natural light.
□

Karl Marx School complex 1930-3

avenue Karl Marx
Villejuif

111

Lurçat won the competition for the school in Villejuif in collaboration with a team of educationalists and hygienists, for he intended the design as a model for schools in a classless society. The classrooms are in a long three-storey block facing a playground to the south. Built of reinforced concrete, the south walls of the classroom block are almost entirely of glass (a comparison with Duiker's Open-air School, Amsterdam (1930) ◇ 263 is interesting). Three covered paths run from this main block, creating two courtyards, a small one for infants and a larger one for boys and girls. A covered play area runs round the courtyards, allowing the children to play even in inclement weather. The kindergarten is in a separate block to the west of the main school.
□

Villeurbanne city centre 1931-4

Place Albert Thomas
Villeurbanne

112

Following World War I, France became the centre for visionary city planning. Tony Garnier's Cité Industrielle, originally conceived in 1904 but first published in 1918, proved a profound inspiration for Le Corbusier's Radiant City and for André Lurçat's plans for the Paris suburb of Villejuif. But the most remarkable scheme ever to be built is by the almost unknown Maurice Leroux in Villeurbanne, next to Lyon. Villeurbanne had grown precipitously from a thinly spread population of 21,000 at the beginning of the century to 85,000 by 1930. In order to unite the disparate hamlets that comprised Villeurbanne, the planners decided to create a new town centre. A broad boulevard flanked by stepped eleven-storey blocks of flats leads up to the stripped Classical city hall designed by Robert Giroud. The entrance to this grand promenade, intended to offer the relief of fresh air in a predominantly industrial city, is marked by grand eighteen-storey skyscraper blocks of flats. The city hall is paired with a large Palace of Public Works in the grand civic square at the end of the boulevard. Both the city hall and the Palace of Public Works are of reinforced concrete construction, while the tall blocks of flats have a steel frame with curtain walls of hollow tile covered by a coating of waterproof cement.
□

137

128

138-139

132-133

156

114-115

116

177-179

157-176

134

113

129-131

144

141

122-124

125-127

140

117-121

145-146

135-136

147-155

142-143

Fagus factory 1911-12

113 The Fagus shoe-last factory, Gropius' first major work, is one of the truly seminal buildings of the twentieth century. At the time, it was decades ahead of typical industrial design and even today it seems contemporary. The young Gropius (he was only twenty years old) received the commission from Carl Benscheidt, who heard Gropius lecture about improving production through a better working environment and received a standard letter from the architect. Gropius took over from the preliminary sketches by Eduard Werner to create his masterpiece.

The structure of the factory is traditional: of masonry with columns in front and a load-bearing wall at the back. Steel beams are used in the floors. But the most striking thing about the factory is the glazed curtain wall of the main three-storey block. The metal frames for the glazing and the solid panels are projected slightly forward from the brick piers, emphasising that it is not a load-bearing wall. The structural bravura is further stressed by the omission of the corner piers: instead the glass hangs in space, enclosing the seemingly unsupported reinforced concrete staircase. The influence of Peter Behrens can be seen in the Fagus factory through the projecting glass wall (recalling the 1909 AEG turbine hall ◇ 159). Gropius, in fact, worked in Behrens' office from 1908 to 1910.
□

Böttcherstrasse 1922-31

architect
Bernhard Hoetger

114 Bremen's Böttcher-strasse is in many ways the first 'theme park' of the twentieth century. Ludwig Roselius, inventor of the caffeine-free 'Coffee HAG', decided soon after World War I to create a tourist attraction in the centre of his native Bremen. By 1923, he had purchased the whole of Böttcherstrasse, a short medieval alleyway near the town hall, and set about refashioning it according to his own visions. He renovated the 1588 Roselius house, then demolished the rest of the street and commissioned several architects to rebuild the street with the requirement that the design reflect the traditional details and materials of Bremen's town centre. The result is a strange amalgam of Jugendstil, vernacular, Expressionist and idiosyncratic architecture. Bernhard Hoetger's two works, the 1922 Paul Becker-Modersohn house and the 1931 Atlantis house, are probably the strangest on the street. The Becker-Modersohn house uses bricks in wild, fanciful decorative patterns, in a composition that climbs upward into a fantastic tower. The ground floor contains shops and an adjoining court has several craft workshops clustered around. The Atlantis house contains a bowling alley, theatre and cinema. The façade, an intricate pattern of concentric circles in brick, was reshaped in 1956 by the sculptor Ewald Matare. But the best part of Atlantis house is an Expressionist spiralling staircase, which seems to be borrowed from the set of an early Fritz Lang film.
□

Neue Vahr apartment building 1958-62

architect
Alvar Aalto

115 The Finnish architect Alvar Aalto is not well known for his few high-rise buildings, but with the Neue Vahr apartments he created one of the best of the post-war housing blocks. The unusual fan-like plan was designed so that one-room studio apartments would have better views through the large windows the fan makes possible. In addition, the fan breaks up the typical monotonous lift corridor in most high-rise blocks, and creates a wide variety of flat plans. The occasionally eccentric plans that result are, in fact, one of the problems with the design, as awkward corners of unusable space sometimes result. Aalto later developed this fan-like form of high rise in his 1965 Schönbühl apartment building in Lucerne, but the grace of the Neue Vahr is compromised in the later work.
□

Sägemühlenstrasse 7-9
Celle

Volksschule 1929

architect

Otto Haesler

116 Haesler trained as a stonemason, but after architectural apprenticeships with Ludwig Bernoully and Hermann Billing he received his first independent commission in Celle, north-east of Hanover. Although he was among the more innovatory architects of his day, Haesler remained in Celle, far from the ferment in Berlin and elsewhere, until driven into hiding by Nazi persecution in 1934 (the Nazis considered Modern architecture 'decadent'). The Volkschule is one of the best examples of Haesler's work in Celle. Twin wings of classrooms flank a covered central hall, which is used both as an assembly hall and gymnasium. Although the exterior windows are not quite in an uninterrupted strip, the supporting wall has been pared down to a minimum, allowing ample natural light into the classrooms. The central hall is lit by a continuous rooflight of glass blocks marching down the central axis. The whole composition, in fact, is rigidly symmetrical. Haesler also designed the blocky, cubic rector's house next door to the school.

☐

Alexandraweg 26
Darmstadt

Ernst Ludwig House 1899-1901

architect

Joseph Maria Olbrich

117 The Ernst Ludwig House, a mixture of artist's studios, bachelor flats and meeting rooms, was the focal point of the artists' colony that Olbrich designed for Ernst Ludwig, the grand duke of Hesse, on the Mathildenhöhe in Darmstadt. A long low building, with a large northern roof-light for the studios, the Ernst Ludwig House has a similar form to Mackintosh's Glasgow School of Art. But Olbrich's approach is, on the whole, less decorative than Mackintosh's and more visibly in a vernacular tradition. The exception to this is the arched entrance, flanked by large sculptures of Man and Woman. One critic has noted that this entrance, with its elaborate <u>Jugendstil</u> decoration, has 'the cultlike overtones of a "temple of work".

☐

Alexandraweg 23
Darmstadt

First Glückert house 1900-1

architect

Joseph Maria Olbrich

119 The first Glückert house is an excellent example of Olbrich's highly decorative Jugendstil, which is overlaid on a fairly traditional-looking house. The arch of the entrance is similar to the arch of the Ernst Ludwig House ◇ 117, but, befitting the domestic nature of this design, the decoration is far more understated, confined to the pointed gold chevrons. The door, however, is richly carved and its shape emphasises the embracing circle of the entrance. Apart from this entrance, the form of the house seems a north German vernacular: bulging gables, however, retain the traditional forms but hint at the restless Jugendstil decoration and impulses the architect has strewn throughout.
☐

Alexandraweg 17
Darmstadt

Own house 1900-1

architect

Peter Behrens

118 Behrens' house for himself on the Mathildenhöhe in Darmstadt was his first building. Part of the artists' colony established by Ernst Ludwig, prince of Hesse, Behrens' house is the only one not designed by the architect Joseph Maria Olbrich. Behrens' house makes an interesting contrast to the more overtly decorative work of Olbrich, but its relatively traditional exterior conceals a lively, Jugendstil influenced interior. The exterior is reminiscent of Behrens' native northern Germany, with its gable, green-glazed moulded bricks in ogival form and pure white rendered walls, and red-tiled roof. Inside the basically cubic volume, the rooms are cleverly packed together: on the ground floor sliding screens open from the entrance hall to the music-room, which is connected to the dining-room through a wide arch. This continuous flow of rooms is similar, though not so advanced, as the planning of Frank Lloyd Wright's contemporary work in the United States. Behrens, who later established himself as a leading industrial designer and graphic designer as well as architect, designed the carpets, wall panels, ceilings, doors, light fittings, furniture, cutlery, glass, china and linen for the house.
☐

Habich house 1900-1

architect

Joseph Maria Olbrich

120 The Habich house is one of Olbrich's more conventional works in the Mathildenhöhe artists' colony, but the simple variations on its symmetrical white façade make it one of the most appealing houses. The façade is of almost Classical symmetry, perhaps a foretaste of the overt Classicism of Olbrich's last works, but this is slightly jarred by the curving lines of the central bay and the sweeping forms of the ironwork balcony. A more typical Olbrich decorative note, at least for this date, is the swirling ironwork of the twin planters that stand on either side of the front door.
☐

Wedding tower and exhibition building 1905-8

architect

Joseph Maria Olbrich

121 The extraordinary wedding tower, one of the most striking images of twentieth-century architecture, and its adjoining exhibition building, mark Olbrich's strong move away from his youthful <u>Jugendstil</u>. The wedding tower recalls the stepped gables of north Germany, but the image is more of a hand reaching its five fingers into the sky. The motif that Olbrich uses to mark the divisions of the tower, the bands of windows that slip around the corners, was to be immensely influential throughout Germany. What Eric Mendelsohn liked about the wedding tower were its 'impregnable surfaces'. The exhibition building is more formal and conventional, arranged atop the municipal reservoir. Its character is Classical, although this is lightened by the large, vernacular-looking roof.
☐

Tietz (now Kaufhof) department store 1906-9

architect

Joseph Maria Olbrich

122 The Tietz department store was one of Olbrich's largest and last works, completed after his death at age forty-one of leukaemia. Although it owes a debt in form to Alfred Messel's earlier Wertheim department store in Berlin, Olbrich's work itself proved influential in the development of the building type throughout the Rhineland. Olbrich's involvement with the Vienna Secession can be glimped still in some of the details, such as the decorative stone carvings, but it is the vaguely Classical look of the building that is most striking. The repetitive vertical elements and the large Mansard-like roof lend the Tietz a certain affluent, bourgeois air, and Olbrich has designed the façade to add weight and strength in the centre of the composition.
□

Mannesmann administration building 1911-12

architect

Peter Behrens

123 The Mannesmann building makes clear Behrens' affinity with Classicism, even more than the great AEG turbine hall ◇ 159 in Berlin. A massive Renaissance palazzo of an office building, the steel-framed construction is clad in stone with a rusticated base of limestone and upper storeys of smooth ashlar. The tall Doric columns flanking the main door make explicit the Classical references. With his first office building, Behrens pioneered an internal arrangement that was to become commonplace later in the century. Faced with a management that was unsure of its internal requirements, Behrens designed a system of open floors, without structural cross walls. Partitions between offices were soundproof and demountable, designed for easy removal and relocation within the grid of internal piers and regularly spaced windows.
□

Heinrich-Heine-Allee
Düsseldorf

Wilhelm-Marx-Haus 1922-4

architect

Wilhelm Kreis

124 Kreis established his reputation before World War I with a series of massive national monuments, but by the twenties he had become far more involved in commercial buildings. The thirteen-storey Wilhelm-Marx-Haus is a good example of the German office building of the time, and makes an interesting comparison with Höger's contemporary Chilehaus in Hamburg ◇ 133. Kreis confined his decoration to the open-work tracery of brick at the top of his tower and a course of shallow arches marking the top of the lower half of the building. It is noticeable that in the work of Kreis and most other German architects in the early twenties, there is almost no attempt to emphasise the verticality of what for their time were tall buildings.

☐

Freiherr-vom-Stein Strasse
Frankfurt am Main

Westend synagogue 1908-10

architect

Franz Roeckle

125 An eclectic work with overtones of the Jugendstil, the Westend synagogue was one of Germany's few major synagogues to survive the Nazi regime. The entrance pavilion with its squat, heavy piers has a brooding character, but the temple itself is a lofty work that combines vaguely Classical details with a more ancient, Middle Eastern aesthetic.

☐

City gas works 1911-13

architect

Peter Behrens

126 The Frankfurt gas works was one of a series of industrial complexes that Behrens designed both before and after World War I. The gas works is composed of a number of fairly small, distinct brick buildings, with forms that recall medieval architecture. The layout was determined by Behrens on functional requirements: buildings are grouped around a railway branch line, with the furnaces at the western end, gasholders at the far eastern end, and between them the processing plant to the south and workshops and offices to the north along Schielestrasse. The most interesting design in the gas works, however, was for the tall cylindrical water tower. Originally, the tower, of brown-glazed brick, was connected to three lower cylindrical towers, each joined by an arched bridge. The three lower towers were for the storage and processing of tar and ammonia, and the entire group was designed within the strictest functional limits: their seeming decorative styling was in fact no more than a thin skin over the required internal facilities. Unfortunately, two of the smaller towers were demolished in 1979.
☐

Generalanzeiger building 1911

architect

Ludwig Bernoully

127 The Generalanzeiger building is among the strongest examples of the massive Doric style prevalent in Germany at the beginning of the century. Peter Behrens was probably its best exponent, but every city in Germany still has examples of the style which is a direct descendant of the nineteenth-century architecture of Schinkel, Gilly and von Klenze, and perhaps laid the ground for the stripped Classicism of Nazi architecture. Bernoully's building has a gently undulating façade of giant order half-columns, with a concentration of massing towards the centre with the Doric half-columns supporting the frieze (which originally proclaimed General-Anzeiger) with rather weak statues above. The addition of a banal steel and glass frontage on the ground floor has unfortunately wrecked some of the impact of Bernoully's composition.
☐

Seestrasse 7 off Route 207
Gut Garkau, near Lübeck

Farm complex 1924-5

architect

Hugo Häring

128 Häring was a leading
theorist of early
Modernism, but few of his projects
were ever built. Justly the most
famous of Häring's works is the
farm complex at Gut Garkau, of
which only the cow shed and barn
were ever completed. The genesis
of the design for such seemingly
banal building types reveals the
depth of Häring's functionalist
convictions: his buildings truly
respond to the needs of the users
both in content and form. The cow
shed had to house forty-two cows,
so Häring concluded that the circle
cows prefer feeding in would
create too much redundant space:
hence the circle became an oval,
which was further modified to a
roughly pear-shaped building to
accommodate the bull. The bull is
given pride of place, segregated at
one end of the shed, but in a
position so that all the cows can
clearly see him (since Häring's
design, experiments have shown
that the presence of a bull
substantially increases the calving
rate of cows). The pear-shaped
plan also allows easy circulation:
milking parlour and both incoming
and outgoing doors are at the
same end, and the dung trough is
continuous. Fodder is supplied
from the hayloft above through a
trapdoor; the feed floor tapers to
take account of the diminishing
amount of feed as it is consumed.
This ingenious plan is matched by
the treatment of the exterior. Brick
infill is clearly distinct from the
reinforced-concrete frame.
□

86 | Ger

Stirnband 10
Hohenhagen, Hagen

Hohenhof 1906-8

architect

Henry van de Velde

129 Hohenhof, the grand house for Karl Ernst Osthaus, was the first house to be built in his self-created artists' colony in Hohenhagen. For his own house, Osthaus chose van de Velde, who had already overhauled Osthaus' Folkwang museum in the centre of Hagen (1901-2, at Hochstrasse 73). Hohenhof sits above a steep valley, the Donnerkuhle, and the house is orientated so the living-room has views down the valley. The walls of the house are of a coursed rubble, from a locally quarried limestone. Smooth black basalt is used for the ashlar facing on the ground floor. The composition of the whole has a picturesque quality, reminiscent of the American shingle style. The ground plan of the main house is L-shaped, with one wing containing the living-room and study, the other the dining-room, nursery and theatre-room. A circular spiral staircase climbs up from the hexagonal hall that acts as a pivot for these two wings. Given the Arts and Crafts ethos of van de Velde, it is unsurprising that a number of artists collaborated on the decoration. Van de Velde himself designed the furniture and most of the decoration, but among the other contributions is a ceramic triptych, <u>Nymph and Satyr</u>, by Henri Matisse in the ground-floor winter garden. The lodge, that juts out at right angles to the main house towards Stirnband, was the home of J. L. M. Lauweriks when he first came to Hagen. Hohenhof has recently been restored as a guest house for official visitors to Hagen.

☐

Hassleyerstrasse 35
Hohenhagen, Hagen

Cuno house 1909-10

architect

Peter Behrens

130 The Cuno house, part of the Hohenhagen development by Karl Ernst Osthaus, is one of Behrens' most rigidly symmetrical works and in its implied Classicism seems to recall the great Prussian architect Schinkel. The rusticated base is topped by rough-cast walls, a division similar to Renaissance palazzos, but the façade is dominated by the glazed central staircase. In its form and detailing, the staircase resembles a fragment of some giant Doric column: the glazing in place of fluting, the cornice in place of a capital. The plan reflects the symmetry of the exterior, but this perfect symmetry seems to have been at the expense of practicality. The living-room faces north-east, preventing almost any sunlight from entering, and the terrace directly overlooks other properties.

The Cuno house is now used as a school building.

☐

Artists' colony houses 1910-14

architect

J.L.M. Lauweriks

131 The Dutch architect Lauweriks is best known for his polemical and theoretical writings in the avant-garde magazines Der Ring, Architectura and Wendingen. Lauweriks was a strong believer in the occult, but his architectural theories were equally strongly rational: his design system was based strictly on regular geometric proportions and shapes. In 1909 Lauweriks, who had just taken up a post at the Düsseldorf School of Arts and Crafts at the invitation of Peter Behrens, moved to Hagen to build his group of houses in Hohenhagen. Like the other works by Behrens and van de Velde in Hohenhagen, Lauweriks' houses were built at the invitation of Karl Ernst Osthaus, who split his land into three to allow the architects to have their freedom.

Lauweriks built a group of six houses (one was a three-family house) on Stirnband. Using his favourite geometric pattern of rectilinear spirals, Lauweriks both planned his small estate and detailed the design of the individual houses. The houses themselves are built up in plan of groups of rectangles, and the group of six advances and recedes in line with the predetermined geometry. Originally, the gardens too followed these spiral patterns. On the houses, the areas of roughly hewn stone contrast with flat areas of brick in a pattern further determined by Lauweriks' geometry.

Of the six houses, probably the most interesting was the earliest, the 1910 Thorn-Prikker house at Stirnband 38.

□

Gänsemarkt
Hamburg

Finance building 1919-26

architect

Fritz Schumacher

132 As chief city architect in Hamburg from 1909 until his forced retirement in 1933, Fritz Schumacher developed a municipal style based on north German traditions that was to leave an indelible imprint on the city. His sober, rectilinear buildings are invariably in the red clinker brick (Backstein) also used by Fritz Höger, but Schumacher's works are far more reticent. The finance building (Finanzbehörde) stands grandly on the corner of the Gänsemarkt, with its round tower smoothly sweeping the eye around the turn of the street. Schumacher was responsible for much of the planning of central Hamburg, and his buildings are of particular interest for their contextual presence: they fit naturally with their surroundings (although some of the post-war architecture of Hamburg has destroyed Schumacher's sensitive placement). Schumacher was aided in his fight for a contextual architecture by the 1912 Baupflegegesetz, a comprehensive planning law which he helped form which regulated building elevations, outdoor signs and advertisements, and conserved trees and buildings and areas of historical and aesthetic value.

□

Chilehaus 1923

architect

Fritz Höger

133

Hamburg was the first European city to experience the impact of the office building in the city centre. The Kontorhaus, the Hamburg forerunner of the modern speculative office building, was designed for internal flexibility: since future tenants were unknown at the time of construction, services such as stairs, lavatories, heating, lightwells, had to be grouped around the centre so the office areas could be divided as required. This building type was combined in Hamburg with a local love for the use of Backstein (clinker brick) to achieve a deep wall texture as well as, through the use of vitrified brick, a wide range of colours. Fritz Höger was the best of the Hamburg architects working in this tradition, and his Chilehaus is the most important product. The great prow of Chilehaus, thrusting into the streets of Hamburg, stands as a symbol of Hamburg's importance as a port. Höger's dramatic shape for Chilehaus was wilful, not conditioned by the site, as it would seem. Fritz Schumacher, Oberbaudirektor in Hamburg, cleared the path for Höger's design through a series of property deals and preferential building permits. The decorative effect of the façade is created by the pattern of the triangular brick piers, with every seventh course laid sideways. This produces a hatching effect when viewed from the side and makes part of the façade seem windowless.

Anzeiger building 1927-8

architect

Fritz Höger

134 Höger never again reached the heights of his 1923 Chilehaus, Hamburg ◇ 133, but throughout his career he continued to explore the uses of his beloved <u>Backstein</u> (clinker brick), which was a traditional material of northern Germany. One of the most unusual results was the Anzeiger building (now the Hannoversche Allgemeine Zeitung building): in an extremely unusual programme, the newspaper offices are crowned by the dome of a planetarium. While the use of <u>Backstein</u> at ground level is successful (almost art deco in its form), the profile of the building resembles a giant orange juice squeezer.
□

Apartments and single-family houses 1901-5

architect

Hermann Billing

135 Hermann Billing, together with Hans Curjel and Karl Moser, developed a distinctive Karlsruhe variety of <u>Jugendstil</u> which simplified the exuberant decoration of others and moulded buildings in plastic shapes. The complex of houses on Baischstrasse shows the inventiveness of Billing at its best: the entrance to the street immediately seems to announce a passage into a different world. The heavy rustication employed by Billing, together with the almost Romanesque details, suggests the influence of the American nineteenth-century architect, Henry Hobson Richardson.
□

Luther church 1907

architect

Hans Curjel and Karl Moser

136 The Luther church is one of the best examples of the modern Karlsruhe school, whose architects in the first decade of the century trod the narrow line between the exuberance of Viennese Secessionism and more traditional, historically based styles. The roughly hewn dark-grey stone of the exterior recalls in its forms the work of Henry Hobson Richardson in the United States, notably his Trinity Church, Boston (1872-7). Richardsonian Romanesque found a natural home in Germany, where the Rundbogenstil (round arch style) stretched back into the Middle Ages. In the Luther church, the use of the Romanesque echoes the sculpted forms of the stone, and the recollection of this old style seems particularly appropriate given the large statue of Luther seemingly carved out of the church's fabric. Of especial interest is the low porte cochère, where the sheer weight of the church's stone seems to press the arches into the ground. This impression is reinforced on the interior, where the gallery rests on stubby, almost medieval columns below the massive, low vault.

□

City hall 1907-11

architect

Hermann Billing

137 Billing won the competition to replace Kiel's Gothic city hall with an eclectic work for the site overlooking a stretch of water and flanked by the city theatre and a bank building. The city hall itself is dominated by the Venice-inspired campanile (Kiel is one of the many self-styled Venices of the North). The stone-clad exterior is richly decorated with vaguely Jugendstil motifs, but this style bursts free from its external sobriety in the interior's central rotunda. North German tradition is more clearly reflected in the three inner courtyards, which are of characteristic clinker brick.

□

Beckergrube 10-14
Lübeck

City theatre 1907-8

architect

Martin Dülfer

138 The Lübeck city theatre is a good example of the peculiar weightiness, the amalgam of details, in Dülfer's work. Established as an expert in theatre design following his city theatre in Dortmund (1903), the massive rough-cut masonry blocks of the Lübeck theatre were Dülfer's principal trademark. He combines this rusticated style with <u>Jugendstil</u> decoration: the figurative frieze is by the Munich artist Georg Römer. Dülfer's style seems idiosyncratic, but it has its roots in the nineteenth-century revival of the <u>Rundbogenstil</u> (German Romanesque) and the works of Friedrich von Thiersch, with whom Dülfer briefly worked, and Theodor Fischer.

☐

Moltkeplatz 1
Lübeck

Villa Stave 1909

architect

Hermann Muthesius

139 Muthesius' importance in architectural history rests more on a series of three books he wrote at the beginning of the century than on any of the buildings he designed. From 1896 to 1903, Muthesius served as an attaché in the German Embassy in London, studying English architecture and design. Out of these studies he wrote a series of books, the most famous of which was <u>Das englische Haus</u> (1904-5). These books had an enormous impact on German domestic architecture, prompting the development of an 'English style,' but they also promoted the concept of <u>Sachlichkeit</u>, or functional, utilitarian design. Muthesius saw the keys to English domestic design as craftsmanship, economy and suitability. The Villa Stave is one of the many houses

Muthesius later built according to these principles, and in its scale and setting it evokes nicely his interpretation of English domestic architecture. The steeply pitched roofs and large chimney clearly mark this as a house, although the proportions probably owe more to the local traditions of Schleswig-Holstein than England. However, the terraces and the hints of Classicism on the first floor are typical of Muthesius' work.

☐

Christ the King church 1926

architect

Dominikus Böhm

Städtisches Museum 1972-82

architect

Hans Hollein

140 Böhm was the leading church architect of his generation in Germany, designing a series of Roman Catholic churches that combine Expressionist forms with a deep understanding of the symbolic and liturgical needs of a church. The entrance, a steep, pointed arch in brick with an adjoining bell tower in brick and concrete, gives only the barest hint of the drama inside the church. A continuous parabolic tunnel-vault in unplastered reinforced concrete stretches over both nave and sanctuary. Lower cross-vaults over the aisles slice into the main vault, creating a seemingly dynamic structure that recalls the finest Gothic cathedrals. Although in an earlier church, St John the Baptist, Neu-Ulm (1921-7), Böhm used a method that dispensed with formwork in the execution of the structure, here the exposed concrete with the lines of the formwork still showing anticipates the Brutalist use of concrete thirty years later.
☐

141 The Mönchengladbach museum, like all of Viennese architect Hans Hollein's works, is a harking back to the crafts-based architecture of the turn-of-the-century Secession. Every detail, every lighting fixture, every piece of fabric has been thought out by Hollein over a ten-year period of building. The care, sometimes agonising, that was taken over the building is reflected in the reported one year it took for completion of the coffee shop, a minuscule portion of the museum. Hollein was fortunate in having a client who selected him for precisely this attention to jewel-like details, and a museum that had a fixed collection of contemporary art. The museum has been designed around this collection: each work of art receives a special setting, a particular view, some special lighting. In its larger conception, the museum has also been designed around the city of Mönchengladbach, for Hollein weaves the main circulation paths of the city into the entrance to the museum. Hence one enters at the top of the museum, which cascades down a steep hill. From there one passes down into the museum, where labyrinthine paths lead around the collection. Despite the constant attention to detail, occasionally Hollein seems to have become preoccupied with his art at the expense of the art hanging on the walls: the use of bare fluorescent tubes for lighting in some parts is particularly unfortunate.
☐

Haus der deutschen Kunst 1933

architect

Paul Ludwig Troost

143 Troost had the dubious distinction of being the first chief architect for Adolf Hitler, and the House of German Art (now the House of Art) was one of the group of official buildings he designed for the Third Reich in the centre of Munich (after Troost's death in 1934, Albert Speer replaced him as Hitler's architect). Apart from the political interest, the architecture of this art gallery marks the beginning of the stripped Classicism that was to characterise Nazi architecture: the long rows of attenuated Doric columns have, in some buildings unfairly, come to be seen as a fingerprint of fascism.
□

Old Anatomy building 1905-7

architect

Max Littmann

142 Littmann is widely known as the leading theatre architect of Munich around the turn of the century, but his most interesting building is the Old Anatomy building for the medical faculty in Munich. An early use of reinforced concrete, the anatomy building is composed of a series of round, shallow-domed operating theatres clustered around the large central theatre.
□

Pilgrimage church 1962-8

architect

Gottfried Böhm

144 Gottfried Böhm, the son of Dominikus Böhm, the great German church architect of the first half of the century, is one of the few Expressionist architects of the sixties and seventies. But he seems to have picked up the style of his father's early churches, such as Christ the King, Mainz-Bischofsheim (1926) ◇ 140, and transformed it into a thoroughly contemporary style. The small town of Neviges has been a place of pilgrimage since 1681, when it was consecrated to the Holy Virgin. The small Gothic chapel, connected to a Franciscan monastery, seats only 200 so in the sixties it was decided to build a larger facility for the 200,000 pilgrims that come to Neviges each year. The church is approached along a wide pilgrims' way, which is flanked by a 100-metre-long concrete wall. The polygonal ground plan and the folded-plate concrete roof seem like a small mountain range that rises to a height of 35 metres. The folds of the plan and the irregular structure shape the large, unadorned interior: all wall surfaces are merely sand-blasted exposed concrete (a further echo of Dominikus Böhm's work). Böhm's mountain-like concrete structure seats 800 with standing room for a further 2,200.
□

Kressengartenstrasse
Nuremberg

Milchhof 1930

architect

Otto Ernst Schweizer

145 One of the most accomplished industrial buildings of its time, the Milchhof centres around the 108-metre-long factory with its clearly defined structure of reinforced concrete. The infill panels are of glazed brick with steel-framed windows above. In the administration building, the offices are arranged around a triple-height atrium. Schweizer's original scheme included associated garages, a canteen building and a keeper's house, all in a consistent style, but unfortunately only the main buildings remain in their original state.
□

Zeppelinstrasse
Nuremberg

Party Congress grounds 1934

architect

Albert Speer

146 Speer became Hitler's personal architect and confidant in 1934, following the death of Paul Ludwig Troost, and the desires and tastes of the two produced a series of massive buildings in Berlin and Nuremberg. Speer's architecture was designed to evoke power, through its references to Imperial Rome as well as through its enormous scale. The buildings were also designed to be effective as ruins: in planning for a 1,000-year Reich, both Hitler and Speer wanted to ensure that buildings endured. The Party Congress Grounds in Nuremberg are already a ruin, fortunately only a few decades after construction, but the effectiveness with which Speer carried out his aims can clearly be seen. The precisely cut stone is slowly crumbling and being covered with weeds, but the simple, bare outlines of the architecture have hardly changed at all. The grounds, however, were designed to be but a backdrop to a larger production: the annual Nazi Party Congress. Speer organised these events like monstrous Gesamtkunstwerken: rows of flags and banners, powerful searchlights cutting shafts in the dark sky and the choreography of the masses all tied in with the inhuman scale of the architecture. ☐

Schlossplatz
Stuttgart

Kunstgebäude 1909-12

architect

Theodor Fischer

147 Theodor Fischer's primary importance in German architecture was as a pedagogue: Dominikus Böhm, Eric Mendelsohn, J. J. P. Oud and Hugo Häring were among his students, Paul Bonatz was his teaching assistant, and Bruno Taut was apprenticed to him during his time in Stuttgart. Himself a student of Friedrich von Thiersch, Fischer was a leading exponent of a revivalist German Classicism. Yet unlike others, Behrens notably, Fischer's Classicism never became weighty and massive, but retained the lightness of southern German vernacular. The Kunstgebäude, on a critical site adjacent to the Neues Schloss and facing the Altes Schloss, well illustrates Fischer's light touch. In monumental surroundings, he designed a reticent building with a delicate gallery of round arches and a shallow cupola above. The stripped-down Doric of Fischer's columns could be related to the stripped Classicism of Behrens and others, but the spindly thinness of the Kunstgebäude is in complete contrast to the powerful Doric of other German architects of the same period. ☐

Gustav-Siegle-Haus 1910-12

architect

Theodor Fischer

148 The Gustav-Siegle-Haus is one of Fischer's most curious works, a mixture of vernacular and his characteristically light Classicism. Built for communal education, it now serves as the home of the Stuttgart School of Music. A large hall which seats 1,000 and three smaller recital halls are its primary facilities. The front has a curious porch of six attentuated Doric columns, but the frieze they support is broken in the middle by an entrance pavilion for the main concert hall.
□

Railway station 1911-28

149 The idea of the railway station as the cathedral of the industrial age was heroically expressed in the nineteenth century by such masterworks as St Pancras Station, London. But Bonatz's heavily rusticated work in Stuttgart is perhaps the twentieth century's greatest expression of this conceit. The rock-faced ashlar and round arches make clear Bonatz's debt to his mentor, Theodor Fischer, but Bonatz's work also resembles the contemporary work of Wilhelm Kreis in Germany and Hendrik Petrus Berlage in Holland.

The Stuttgart station is notable primarily for its external appearance: the enormous clock tower aiding hurrying travellers, the clearly expressed central hall, the giant arch spewing out passengers during the rush hour. Inside, the waiting-hall has massive concrete beams supporting the roof far above milling crowds. The train sheds of 1924 are far less interesting.

□

Dorotheenstrasse/Münzstrasse
Stuttgart

Market hall 1912-14

architect

Martin Elsaesser

150 Stuttgart's large covered market from the outside looks a traditional building: the low arches marching along the façade, ending in an old round tower. But inside, a light, airy hall spanned by side-reinforced concrete arches opens up. Elsaesser's design combines traditional elements with modern constructional techniques. The wide pointed arches along the ground floor make clear the hall's affinity with the nearby medieval works, the Stiftskirche and the Altes Schloss. The form, too, of the hall is like a medieval basilica: the large rectangular space with the vaults above and natural light from clerestory windows. Elsaesser takes advantage of his concrete construction, however, and brings a further flood of natural light into the hall through his almost continuous series of roof-lights. Years later, in 1927-8, Elsaesser designed the massive central market for Frankfurt am Main without concealing his Modernist impulses on the exterior.

□

Bruckmannweg,
Rathenaustrasse Stuttgart

Single and twin houses 1927

architect

Le Corbusier

151 The two buildings Le Corbusier built for the Weissenhof exhibition were probably the most consciously geared to develop the stated theme of a new way of life in the 'New Dwelling'. The single-family house, at the base of Bruckmannweg, is a variation of the second Citrohan house project of 1922. The house stands on pilotis, Le Corbusier's characteristic free-standing piers of reinforced concrete, which here are particularly appropriate given the sloping site. Above these, the house basically consists of a double-height living-room with a full-height window wall. The dining-room is to the rear, under the balcony which contained the parents' bedroom. On the top floor are two small bedrooms for a child and guest and a roof terrace. As always, views from the terrace are not completely unobstructed, for Le Corbusier frames the view with the sliced open wall (the framing device almost seems like a Modernist cornice for the house).

The twin houses, on Rathenaustrasse, were, according to Le Corbusier, inspired by a Pullman sleeping-car. Again the houses stand on pilotis, but above these the house is a stretched slab with a long strip window that runs corner to corner illuminating the interior. The interior was basically one large room, which Le Corbusier intended to be subdivided at night with movable partitions. The simple rectangular box is only broken by a small rear extension which houses a breakfast room on the first floor, the staircase, and a small library on the second floor. The main body of the house above the large linear room becomes the sun terrace, which again uses a framing element for views outward. Interestingly, Le Corbusier's two works on the Weissenhof were the most ample and expensive housing in the exhibition.

□

Am Weissenhof 14-20 (evens)
Stuttgart

Housing 1927

architect

Ludwig Mies van der Rohe

152 Mies organised the 1927
Weissenhof Siedlung, and his block
of housing was the largest single element of
the exhibition. The long slab at the crest of the
hill on which the exhibition was built is the only
apartment building in the complex. Because of
the fairly generous budget for the Siedlung,
supplied by the city of Stuttgart out of funds
intended for community housing, Mies was
able to use a steel skeleton structure for his
block. As a result, the strip windows are large
and, importantly, the interior has a minimum of
structural partitions. Since the Weissenhof was
intended as a polemical exhibition of the 'New
Dwelling', Mies and the other participating
architects furnished their interiors. It was at
the Weissenhof that Mies presented the first of
his tubular-steel chairs. The living-rooms in

Mies' block also employed movable veneered
partitions, an idea he developed further in the
Barcelona pavilion in 1929.

□

Pankokweg 1-9 (odds)
Stuttgart

Housing 1927

architect

J. J. P. Oud

153 Oud's work for the Weissenhof
exhibition, a row of five terrace
houses, was perhaps the most minimal of the
designs presented. Given his early affinity with
the De Stijl movement, it is not surprising that
Oud felt that proportion and form was the
essence of architecture and that little more
was required. Today, Oud's row of houses
seems to exhibit many of the faults some
ascribe to Modern architecture: the concrete
has not weathered well, and the houses seem
mean rather than lyrical. But at the time, Oud's
work was considered possibly the most
sophisticated. In the catalogue for the 1932
exhibition at New York's Museum of Modern
Art, Henry-Russell Hitchcock wrote that Oud
was 'the most conscientious of modern
architects. In any period he would have been a

very great architect, in our own he is of all
great architects the most sound.'

□

Hölzelweg 1
Stuttgart

Single-family house 1927

architect

Hans Scharoun

154 Scharoun's house in the Weissenhof <u>Siedlung</u> is exceptional in its deviation from the rectilinear forms of the other buildings. Under the direction of Mies van der Rohe, the Weissenhof was populated with what later came to be seen as the giants of the International style, and Scharoun's conviction that form should follow function independent of any external aesthetic conditions (right angles and flat surfaces, for example) must have seemed heresy amongst the keepers of the true faith. The small detached house in reinforced concrete was one of Scharoun's first important built works, but already his interest in internal planning is evident. As with Le Corbusier's houses nearby ◇ 151, Scharoun's living-room is the centre of the house, visually connected to the other spaces in a free-flowing plan.

☐

Konrad Adenauer Weg
Stuttgart .

Staatsmuseum 1984

architect

James Stirling

155 Stirling's Staatsmuseum marks the resurgence of monumental Classicism in twentieth-century architecture. A vast building, cut into a hillside, the programme includes galleries, a music academy, workshop theatre and lecture theatre. The whole is stitched together in a composition of varied elements and details, dominated by a large central drum that acts as pivot for the major spaces and an almost ceremonial circulation space. Various paths wind the visitor through the building: a ramp takes one up to the entrance hall, one then passes through the glazed entrance space to the grand central drum, and then another ramp takes one up to the galleries which are arranged in series in very proper nineteenth-century style. Stirling enlivens the massive structure with odd construction details (Mannerist slipped stones, Classical portals, exposed steel canopies) and almost vulgar colours: bright green for the entrance wall, pink and blue handrails.

☐

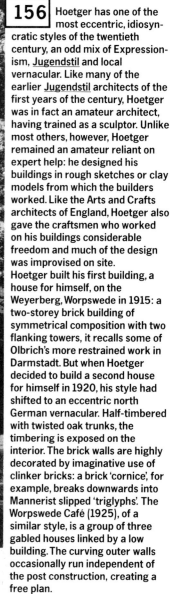

Weyerberg
Worpswede, near Bremen

Own houses, café and exhibition building 1915-27

architect

Bernhard Hoetger

156 Hoetger has one of the most eccentric, idiosyncratic styles of the twentieth century, an odd mix of Expressionism, Jugendstil and local vernacular. Like many of the earlier Jugendstil architects of the first years of the century, Hoetger was in fact an amateur architect, having trained as a sculptor. Unlike most others, however, Hoetger remained an amateur reliant on expert help: he designed his buildings in rough sketches or clay models from which the builders worked. Like the Arts and Crafts architects of England, Hoetger also gave the craftsmen who worked on his buildings considerable freedom and much of the design was improvised on site.
Hoetger built his first building, a house for himself, on the Weyerberg, Worpswede in 1915: a two-storey brick building of symmetrical composition with two flanking towers, it recalls some of Olbrich's more restrained work in Darmstadt. But when Hoetger decided to build a second house for himself in 1920, his style had shifted to an eccentric north German vernacular. Half-timbered with twisted oak trunks, the timbering is exposed on the interior. The brick walls are highly decorated by imaginative use of clinker bricks: a brick 'cornice', for example, breaks downwards into Mannerist slipped 'triglyphs'. The Worpswede Café (1925), of a similar style, is a group of three gabled houses linked by a low building. The curving outer walls occasionally run independent of the post construction, creating a free plan.
□

Steinplatz housing 1906-7

architect

August Endell

157 August Endell was the most famous, and probably the most articulate, of the German Jugendstil architects. His ideas were clearly set out early in his career in the 1896 pamphlet Um die Schönheit, in which he advocated yielding to the emotional content of art rather than relying on intellect. Beauty, he wrote, could be found in nature, particularly in flowers. These theories were elaborated over the years, but Endell's faith in them can be seen in the Steinplatz housing built a decade after he wrote his first pamphlet. The building itself is a fairly typical Berlin apartment block of the era, with one roof embracing both front and back wings. Endell's decoration, however, all on floral motifs, sets it apart from other Berlin blocks of this type. Characteristic of Endell is the slightly macabre rigidity and symmetry of his decoration: it is worlds distant from the lighter, more free-flowing floral decoration of Mackintosh or Guimard. Endell's individuality was fiercely held: in the famous 1914 debate over standardisation versus individualism between Hermann Muthesius and Henry van de Velde, Endell was a vocal supporter of the latter, rejecting Muthesius' idea of homogenous cultural style.
□

Hebbel theatre 1907

architect

Oskar Kaufmann

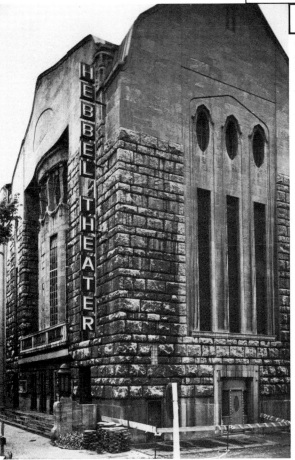

158 Kaufmann was the leading theatre designer of his generation in Germany. Although born in Hungary, Kaufmann came to Karlsruhe to study architecture and eventually formed a practice in Berlin. His most famous work, the 1913 Freie Volksbühne in what is now East Berlin, was destroyed during the war and rebuilt in debased form. His first theatre, however, the Hebbel theatre, survived externally and is a good representation of Kaufmann's style. Like Dülfer's theatre in Lübeck ◇ 138, the Hebbel theatre is heavily rusticated with massive roughly-hewn ashlar. Above this base, forms are vaguely Jugendstil, but more accurately idiosyncratic. Kaufmann was noted for his eccentric, rich interior decoration, but the interior of the Hebbel theatre has been altered from the original.
□

AEG turbine factory 1909-10

architect

Peter Behrens

159 The turbine factory was Behrens' first major building for the German industrial combine AEG, for whom, as artistic consultant, he designed numerous buildings, electrical appliances, catalogues, letterheads, exhibitions and advertisements. Behrens' work for the AEG is one of the first examples of what is now called designing a corporate image. In the course of his work for AEG, Behrens designed many factory buildings, but it is the Moabit turbine factory that most distinctively established Behrens' industrial style.

The turbine factory is built of poured concrete and exposed steel, which are both clearly expressed. A long glass and steel elevation along Berlichingenstrasse allows natural light on to the shop floor, but the most striking feature of the factory is the temple-like front elevation. An enormous 'pediment', with a frieze announcing the AEG Turbinenfabrik caps the 'rusticated' (scored concrete) columns with a central 'void' implied by the planar glass and steel window.

Critical reaction to the turbine factory provides an interesting example of the shift in tastes in the last few decades. Hitchcock, in his Pelican history of nineteenth- and twentieth-century architecture, finds the end elevation less successful than the more industrial side elevation. With renewed interest in the Classical tradition from the mid-seventies, critics can now view the temple end as Behrens' acknowledgement of the antidecorative Doric tradition in German architecture.
□

Bürnerstrasse
Neukölln, West Berlin

Housing 1910

architect

Bruno Taut

160 Bruno Taut was a pivotal figure in the growth of Modern architecture, as the leading member first of the <u>Gläserne Kette</u>, then of <u>Arbeitsrat der Kunst</u> after World War I and then of <u>Der Ring</u> in the twenties. But while Taut would later become clearly identified with first Expressionism and then the International style, his early work is less easily placed. The large block of flats in Neukölln shows some of the influence of the <u>Jugendstil</u> on Taut in its undulating balconies. Taut, however, is far more sparing in his decorative flourishes than <u>Jugendstil</u> architects like August Endell: simple red ceramic tiles on the balconies are the only applied decoration.

☐

Peter-Lenne-Strasse 28-30
Dahlem, West Berlin

Wiegand house 1911-12

architect

Peter Behrens

161 The Wiegand house, Behrens' most overtly Classical work, shows clearly the influence of Schinkel and the client Dr Theodor Wiegand, at the time Germany's most prominent Classical archaeologist. But Behrens' Classicism here, as elsewhere, is not academic as can be seen in the remarkable peristyle at the entrance. The Doric columns are completely unadorned, stripped of fluting and without entasis. The entablature the columns carry is honed to the essentials: a bare architrave, no frieze and a cornice resting on a thick moulding. The peristyle is roofed in glass blocks. The house itself is of ashlar, with a roof of red Roman tiles. The interior has an essentially symmetrical plan, if the service wing to the north-west (wholly integrated with the house from the outside) is discounted. A pergola leads from the ground-floor dining-room to an open pavilion overlooking the garden. Behrens was also responsible for the heavy, solid furniture and decorations in the house. Restored in 1978, the Wiegand house is now the headquarters of the German Archaeological Institute.

☐

Heerstrasse 107
Charlottenburg, West Berlin

Dr Sternefeld house 1923

architect

Eric Mendelsohn

162 The Sternefeld house was one of the first unadorned, cubic buildings in Berlin. A mixture of reinforced concrete and brick construction, the three floors of the house are stacked one atop the other, like a child's building blocks. The smooth surfaces of the rendered walls are sliced at junctions between floors by protruding courses of brick. The original interior plan was fairly conventional with rooms grouped to overlook the garden and bedrooms above opening on to terraces. The house has now been split into four maisonettes and is used as a private old people's home.

☐

Fritz-Reuter-Allee
Britz, West Berlin

Gross-Siedlung Britz 1925-31

architect

Bruno Taut

163 The Siedlung at Britz is one of the best period examples of the interweaving of Modern architecture with nature. The centrepiece of the development is a large horseshoe of three-storey flats, built around a central garden and pond. Each flat has a terrace overlooking this public park, and ground-floor flats have private gardens extending radially toward the centre. Closing off the horseshoe is a small terrace of shops, emphasising the public nature of the project. Elsewhere at Britz, the relationship between architecture and nature is not quite so grand, but alleys of lush gardens stretch between the linear blocks of housing throughout. Bruno Taut was responsible for the bulk of the design at Britz, but Martin Wagner, in addition to work on the overall planning, designed the file of housing with rounded stair-towers on Stavenhagenerstrasse. Bruno Taut's brother, Max Taut, was architect for a small group of flats to the west of Paster-Behrensstrasse, Eduard Ludwig for the housing south of Talbergerstrasse and Bruno Schneidereit for the lines of housing east of Malchinerstrasse.

☐

Lehniner Platz complex 1926-8

architect

Eric Mendelsohn

164 The complex of buildings on Lehniner Platz was Mendelsohn's largest and best work of his early years in Berlin. Included in the project were the Universum cinema (now Schaubühne theatre), a cabaret, restaurant, a hotel and a block of housing. The curved prow of the Universum cinema sweeps visitors into the site, drawing them toward the flats at the back. The curve of the cinema is counterpoised by the blunter lines of the cabaret and restaurant building next door. But everything in Mendelsohn's design emphasises sweeping horizontal lines: the smooth curves of brick, the cinema's unbroken arc of windows, the corner balconies of the housing on Cicerostrasse. Mendelsohn did not neglect the interiors, but unfortunately the greatest example of his interior work, the cinema, has been completely destroyed. Built during the heyday of the silent film, the Universum cinema's interior reflected the sweeping lines of the exterior: the balcony arched around the cinema, lighting created curved, streamlined corners. The cinema was badly damaged during the war, then dreadfully refurbished as a couple of cinemas. In the late seventies, the Senate of Berlin funded reconstruction of the cinema, under the direction of architect Jürgen Sawede: the exterior has been magnificently restored to its original state, but at the price of the complete and irreversible destruction of the interior to create a supposedly flexible, modern theatre.
□

Gross-Siedlung Onkel-Toms-Hütte 1926-31

architect

Bruno Taut

165 The mid- to late-twenties saw tremendous advances in housing design in Berlin, partly because of the numerous opportunities avant-garde architects had to build. The Siedlung, or housing estates, were springing up in every quarter of the city, funded by non-profit-making housing associations to provide mass housing for the workers of Berlin. Taut's particular skill in housing, demonstrated both at Onkel-Toms-Hütte and Britz ◇ 163, was to interweave Modern architecture — the style of the Neue Sachlichkeit — with nature. As at most of the Siedlungen, Taut shared the design with a number of other architects: Taut was in charge of planning, and Hugo Häring and Otto Rudolf Salvisberg designed part of the development. In the five years of construction, more than 10,000 units of housing were erected at Onkel-Toms-Hütte. The basic plan of the development was for long-perimeter blocks of housing, with extensive gardens behind. Streets are tree-lined, but Taut also designed an alternative pedestrian path through the back gardens, isolated from vehicular traffic. Adjoining the development of Onkel-Toms-Hütte is the contemporary Siedlung Fischtalgrund along Am Fischtal, which consists of small groups of houses, or even single-family houses, designed variously by a group of twenty architects. Siedlung Fischtalgrund, with its more traditional housing types, now seems to presage the reactionary backlash against Modern architecture during the Nazi regime.
☐

Titania Palace 1927

architect

Schöffler and Schloenbach

166 The Titania Palace is a good example of the typical giant cinemas of the twenties. The block-like art deco forms of the Titania make an interesting contrast with the curvilinear sweep of Mendelsohn's contemporary Universum cinema ◇ 164. Some unfortunate external alterations have been made, especially at street level, and the interior was remodelled in 1953 by Hermann Fehling.
☐

Single-family house 1928

architect

Wassili and Hans Luckhardt

167 The Luckhardts' house on the Rupenhorn is next door to a twin house designed and built at the same time by the same architects. Before World War I the Luckhardts were associated with Bruno Taut's Expressionist group, the Gläserne Kette, but by the mid-twenties they had become converts to the Neue Sachlichkeit (new objectivity): unadorned planar surfaces, flat roofs, right angles. The 1928 houses show the Luckhardts' best work: their steel-frame construction was innovatory in domestic architecture, and the large expanses of glass were still rare at this date. Both houses are made up of the same basic elements. The ground floor contains all the service rooms, while the first floor is entirely taken up by the living-room, which lets out through sliding glass doors on to a large terrace. Bedrooms are above, and a roof terrace caps the house. Views from the roof terrace are framed by a modern 'cornice' in the manner of Le Corbusier's early houses.
□

German Metal Workers' Union building 1928-9

architect

Eric Mendelsohn

168 Mendelsohn's work of the twenties reflects his almost visionary obsession with strong, flowing lines, clearly seen in his evocative wartime sketches in heavy pencil or charcoal. The organic forms of his early work, notably the 1919 Einstein Tower in Potsdam, give way to clean, streamlined images. The Metal Workers' Union building is a structure of reinforced concrete that plays with the collisions of straight lines and curves. The entrance stands on a corner, and Mendelsohn created a shallow concave front to face the street and to draw visitors in. The concave front block acts as a hinge for the straight wings of offices that radiate along the sides of the triangular site. At the back of the concave front block, a large concrete spiral staircase soars up a glazed stair-hall.
□

Elektro-Mechanik factory 1928

architect

Martin Punitzer

169 A fine example of an early Modern Movement factory by one of Berlin's lesser-known architects. The unbroken bands of windows around the factory give ample natural light to the ground-floor workshops and the offices on the first floor. Heavy machinery was confined to the basement, so the slightly raised platform of the factory allows light into the basement. One of the more unusual aspects of the factory is the light-green tile cladding.
□

Gross-Siedlung Siemensstadt 1929-31

architect

Hans Scharoun et al.

170 The Siemensstadt Siedlung, which was planned by Hans Scharoun, makes an interesting contrast to the contemporary Siedlungen in Berlin planned by Bruno Taut, such as Britz ◇ 163 and Onkel-Toms-Hütte ◇ 165. Scharoun's plan has none of the stitching together of architecture and nature, but is instead a series of individual architectural monuments. Scharoun's own housing at Siemensstadt (shown) is the best work of the development. The flat, white surfaces of the concrete blocks are smoothly broken by the curving protrusion of the terraces. The internal planning of Scharoun's buildings is also of interest: central living/dining areas also serve as key circulation space, eliminating corridors with a series of doors running off. Scharoun's agility in internal planning proved valuable during the Nazi era, when, forced to conform to prescribed vernacular externally, he reserved his Expressionist impulses for innovatory internal plans. Among the many other works at Siemensstadt, of particular interest are Otto Bartning's plain, long curving line of housing along the south side of Goebelstrasse, the recently renovated blocks by Häring along the north side of Goebelstrasse, and the long, strictly conventional Modern block by Gropius on the north-west corner of the intersection of Jungfernheideweg and Goebelstrasse.
□

Breitenbachplatz
Wilmersdorf, West Berlin

Prussian Mines' Administration building 1929-30

architect
Max Taut

171 Max Taut's Prussian Mines building is among the most successful office buildings of the early Modern Movement. The steel skeleton structure is clearly expressed by the large ceramic tiles, while small clinker bricks clad the walls. A magnificent spiral stair of reinforced concrete in a glazed stair-tower at the back links Taut's work with the exactly contemporary Metal Workers' building by Mendelsohn in Kreuzberg ◇ 168.
□

Lepsiusstrasse 112
Steglitz, West Berlin

Ziegler house 1936

architect
Hugo Häring

172 Häring was one of the few true functionalist architects: his oddly shaped buildings derived from the actual living and working patterns of the users; form truly followed function. A prolific writer, Häring took a strong stand against what he saw as the arbitrary geometricism of architects like Le Corbusier. Hence the unusual angled form of the Ziegler house was a response to the inhabitants' way of life. The angle allows the living/dining-room to stretch across the entire garden façade of the house. The ground-level basement is constructed of concrete, while uniform courses of paired bricks clad the upper floors. A winter garden has been built on recently adjoining the living-room.
□

Unité d'habitation 1956-8

architect

Le Corbusier

173 The Berlin Unité, built for the 1957 Interbau exhibition, was the third of Le Corbusier's Unités d'habitation ◇ 63. But the Berlin example contains many of the faults of the original in Marseilles with few of its signs of invention: for example, the sculptural landscape of the Marseilles roof is in Berlin regularised and stripped of its plastic forms. And some of the aspects of the Unité that made some sense in Marseilles, the brise-soleil (concrete sunbreaks) notably, are mere conceits in the normally grey weather of Berlin. As in Marseilles, the immense block of 527 housing units in eighteen storeys is a landmark (or blot, depending on your opinion) in the landscape for miles around. To be fair to Le Corbusier, however, he himself disowned the Berlin Unité because of the terrible work of the builders: his elevational drawings, in particular, were apparently virtually ignored. □

Bartning addition 1957

architect

Hans Scharoun

174 One of the best examples of Scharoun's formal inventiveness from his later work. An addition to the long curving wall of Otto Bartning's housing for the 1929-31 Siedlung (which Scharoun was in charge of), Scharoun's sawtoothed building almost seems like a fanged head for Bartning's serpent. Characteristically, however, Scharoun's plan did not derive from dry formalism, but from the ingenious plans of his apartments. Since the wall along the street is straight, services (kitchen, toilet, breakfast-nook) range along it. The living spaces, therefore, are cranked out, providing all apartments with views and ventilation along two walls. Larger end apartments have cantilevered balconies. □

Berlin Philharmonic Hall 1959-63

architect

Hans Scharoun

175 Scharoun is a rarity in that, in the course of a long career, he remained constant to the Expressionist style of his youth. The Philharmonic, known in Berlin as Karajan's Circus after the Philharmonic's music director and the shape of the hall, is the best of Scharoun's late works. The unusual form, resembling a giant circus tent covered in gold and yellow, derives from the internal requirements: Scharoun seems to drape the exterior of the building thinly over the bulges and angles of the interior. For the interior of the concert hall is far from typical. The orchestra sits in the middle of the hall, with irregularly shaped tiers of seating rising up on all sides. The 2,200 seats are under the folds of the concrete roof, which is itself decorated with an aluminium sculpture by Hans Uhlmann. The result of the unusual shape of the hall and the roof is an excellent acoustic for orchestras: some observers have suggested that the complex shapes of Scharoun's architecture are a modern-day substitute for ornate sculptures and carvings in a nineteenth-century concert hall. The foyers to the concert hall are dominated by a cascading grand staircase, a device that became a trademark of Scharoun's late work. □

Potsdamerstrasse
Tiergarten, West Berlin

Neue Nationalgalerie 1965-8

architect

Ludwig Mies van der Rohe

176 Mies van der Rohe left Germany in 1933, after the Nazis forced the closing of the Bauhaus, and, after a short sojourn in Switzerland, found his way to Chicago and a prolific career in the United States as architect and educator. But it is appropriate that his last work, the New National Gallery, completed shortly before his death, was in the city that spawned him and the other giants of the Modern Movement. The gallery makes explicit the Classical tendencies always present in Mies' work, for it is visibly a temple of the arts, standing on its concrete podium. Its square steel roof, at the time the largest rigid plate ever made, is supported at its edges by two cruciform columns on each side. A recessed glass wall encloses the upper floor of the gallery, which was intended to be

divided by exhibition wall-panels suspended from the roof girders. The main exhibition spaces are at basement level, however, and open on one side to a sculpture court. The New National Gallery is one of Mies' purest statements, but it reveals the failings of his absolutist style in that it has proved very poor for the exhibition of paintings, which require carefully controlled lighting conditions.

☐

Am Zirkus 1
Mitte, East Berlin

Grosses Schauspielhaus 1919

architect

Hans Poelzig

177 The Grosses Schauspielhaus (Great Theatre) was one of the major built works of the Expressionists. The great director Max Reinhardt had bought the dilapidated Schumann Circus building to convert into his own theatre. Reinhardt had two requirements for his theatre: he wanted a panoramic stage 30 metres wide, and a dome to vault the auditorium and arena as the sky vaulted the classical theatre. This dome could not, of course, cover the stage and its tower. He also decided to retain the fabric of the old building. As a result the giant planar walls of the exterior are barely decorated with the tall blind arches that once adorned all the external surfaces. Now a uniform dark red, under Poelzig's original design the red of the façade lightened toward the top, and the blind arches

were distinguished from the wall surface through a change in tonal values. The remarkable interior, unfortunately destroyed during the war, echoed and intensified the decoration of the exterior. The blind arches were transmuted into wired plaster stalactites that dripped down from the ceiling in vast circular courses over the auditorium. The structural columns fanned upwards, like bizarre palmate capitals. The whole cave-like interior was like a giant Expressionist stage set: Poelzig, in fact, designed a number of film sets, including that for the 1920 The Golem, directed by Paul Wegener.

☐

Marie-Curie-Allee
Lichtenberg, East Berlin

Sonnenhof housing 1926-7

architect

Erwin Gutkind

178 The Sonnenhof housing is a
particularly good early example of
modern workers' housing on a corner site.
Unlike some contemporaries, Gutkind here
shunned the taut skin of concrete and glass,
instead emphasising through the varying
horizontal bands the elements of the building.
The reinforced concrete structure is clearly
expressed as the base slab for each floor:
brick infill is then in exposed bands and white
render, stressing the lines of windows. The top
floor is a late addition, as Gutkind capped his
building with a tall attic-storey of brick. The
corner terraces that have been closed are also
late alterations.
□

Oberseestrasse 60
Weissensee, East Berlin

Lemke house 1932

architect

Ludwig Mies van der Rohe

179 The Lemke house was the last of
Mies' works completed before the
Nazis closed the Bauhaus, and in the purity of
its forms and plans is one of the best surviving
early works. The single-storey L-shaped house
is constructed of brick around a small terrace
to the south-west, overlooking a garden and
small lake. Glass walls with full-height doors
open on to the terrace. The living-room
stretches along one side of the terrace, a
studio along the other; the kitchen lies along
the street side, while the small bedroom and
adjoining bathroom are entered from the
studio.
□

UIDE

ARCHITECTURE

Great Britain

198

193-196

242

250

201

184

239

249

200 199

244

205

255 202

181 187-188 203

185

182 241 240

245-247 204 186

190 197

243 180

253 254 206-238

256 251 189

252 183

248

191 192

High and Over 1929

Highover Park
Amersham, Buckinghamshire

180

architect
Amyas Connell

High and Over, built for the former director of the British School in Rome, is the first example of Modern Movement domestic architecture in Britain. The house uses a concrete frame and rendered brick infill and has an unusual Y-shaped plan, more reminiscent of the Beaux Arts than of early Modernism. Strip windows, following the example of Le Corbusier, are used, but the most interesting external feature is the oversailing roof canopy supported between two expressed columns. Inside, the central hexagonal space provides a grand focus for the house, but the division into so many wings seems a bit contrived.
□

Boots' factory 1932

Humber Road South Beeston, Nottinghamshire	**181**	architect **Owen Williams**

The Boots' factory is probably the one building in Britain that could match Continental examples for innovation in engineering and design: its most obvious counterparts are Gropius' Bauhaus and van de Vlugt and Brinkman's Van Nelle factory ◇ 275.

An immense building of reinforced concrete, the distinguishing element of the Boots' factory is the smooth, unbroken glass curtain wall that wraps the entire structure. The concrete mushroom-slab construction steps the structural piers back from the façade allowing the unobstructed glass wall. The glass panes themselves are fixed in steel frames and secured with aluminium strips: on each floor the curtain wall is divided horizontally into three strips, an upper and lower strip of rough-cast glass and a centre strip of polished plate glass. Another innovation was the cantilevered roof over the loading dock which runs the entire 170 metres of the south front, projecting nearly 10 metres out from the bulk of the building. The interior is dominated by the vast atrium of the packing hall, which allows easy internal transport of packing materials both horizontally and vertically.
□

Besford Court 1912-14

architect **A. Randall Wells**	Besford near Pershore, Worcestershire	**182**

Wells, one of the most inventive and least-known architects of the first years of the century, acted as clerk of works at Lethaby's Brockhampton church ◇ 185. This background, combined with the evident influence of Lutyens, produced his additions to the timber-framed fifteenth-century Besford Court. For Sir George Noble and Lady Noble (who Wells married in 1917) Wells gutted the old house to create his new work of stone. The neo-Tudor south front is composed of three canted bay windows on the ground floor and two first-floor oriels in alternate rhythm above. Through a gateway one enters a rather bleak cloister opening on to a timber-studded medieval wall. The grand main staircase surges upwards from this cloister: in stone, and snaking through and around the bulges of the house, the staircase is reminiscent of Lutyens. The Great Hall recalls Wells' own work at Brockhampton, with its pointed transverse arches.
□

De la Warr Pavilion 1933-5

Bexhill-on-Sea, Sussex

183

architect
Mendelsohn and Chermayeff

The largest, and the most characteristic, of the several buildings designed by Mendelsohn during his few years in England after fleeing Nazi Germany. Mendelsohn and Chermayeff won the competition for the pavilion with a long, low Modern building that presents an almost entirely glazed façade to the seaside. A library, restaurant and hall are part of the complex, but the most outstanding feature is the circular, glass-enclosed reinforced concrete staircase which dramatically juts out from the basically box-like confines of the building.
□

Casino 1938-9

Blackpool Pleasure Beach
Blackpool, Lancashire

184

architect
Joseph Emberton

The sweeping white, reinforced concrete circle of the Blackpool Casino is one of the most striking achievements of British 1930s architecture. With its construction and planning, it stands firmly in the Modern Movement tradition, but the forms it evokes relate more to Miami Beach <u>Moderne</u> than to Le Corbusier. The tall tower with its corkscrew of concrete is the visible sign of the Casino, pulling in visitors from afar. By the grand enclosed staircase tower is the main entrance. The large proportions of the staircase were designed to take the crowds of holiday-makers to all the principal public rooms. Constructed of reinforced concrete, it is finished in a light-coloured terrazzo with a black edging to each step. The metal balustrade supports tubular handrails, one ivory coloured, the other tomato red. The ground floor contains the main restaurants, with a banqueting room on the first floor, and a large sun-terrace on the flat roof.
□

Belvedere Road
Burnham-on-Crouch, Essex | **186**

architect

Joseph Emberton

A spare steel-framed structure standing on a reinforced concrete base, Emberton's yacht club is one of the most successful early Modern works in Britain. The whole of the south front, facing the river, is glazed with steel casements, the stanchions being set back to allow unobstructed views both up and down the river. In contrast, the north-facing walls, which are exposed to the prevailing cold winds, are almost entirely solid in order to minimise heat loss. A jaunty concrete spiral staircase climbs to the umpire's box with its cantilevered balcony at the top of the club.

☐

All Saints' Church 1901-2

architect

William Lethaby

Brockhampton
near Ross-on-Wye, Hereford | **185**

Like the other great Arts and Crafts church, St Mary the Virgin, Great Warley (1902-4) ◇ 197, at first glimpse All Saints' Church seems a fairly traditional thatched church. Walls and buttresses are of rubble, and the quoins are roughly chiselled. Inside, however, tradition is banished. Large single chamfered arches spring from the low walls, supporting a concrete tunnel vault. The thatched covering to this concrete vault, although unusual, provides excellent insulation. External simplicity is echoed by the spareness of the interior, but this serves as a perfect foil for the richness of what decoration exists. Tapestries are by Burne-Jones, woven by Morris & Co., and Christopher Whall designed the stained glass. Lethaby himself is responsible for the simple,

Shakeresque furniture and lamps, as well as the fine stone font with its floral carving. Randall Wells acted as clerk of works in Brockhampton, and the clear influence of the church on E. S. Prior's church in Roker ◇ 250 may well have been through Wells, who was clerk of works there as well.

☐

History Faculty building 1964-8

Sidgwick Avenue
Cambridge

187

architect **James Stirling**

The History Faculty shares much of the vocabulary of the earlier, and perhaps more successful, Engineering Faculty in Leicester ◇ 205: hard red brick and large expanses of glazing. The Cambridge work is also clearly ordered in its division of different spaces. A seven-storey L-shaped block contains offices and small study-rooms. The two wings of the L embrace the large cascade of glass under which lies the main reading-room of the library. This tent-like expanse of glass has caused a number of problems since completion, most notably the solar heat gain that makes students swelter in the library for reasons other than exam pressure. Under this glass roof lies in effect a second exterior, for the corridors of the L-shaped block are glazed and overlook the reading-room. The building sits on its own raised plaza and the scale is curiously small: there is an eerie sense that one is seeing a 3/4-scale model.

□

Cripps Building 1967

St John's College
Cambridge

188

architect **Powell & Moya**

The snaking line of the Cripps Building is probably the best of the many college buildings designed in the enormous expansion of British universities in the sixties and early seventies. Its clearly expressed concrete structure, a simple composition of horizontals and verticals, became the model for a number of university hostels, up to the Sir Thomas White Building by Arup Associates at St John's College, Oxford (1975) ◇ 246. The Cripps Building consists of 200 rooms, mostly for undergraduates, with eight larger sets of rooms for fellows. The zigzag four-storey block winds through the grounds of the college, giving views of Lutyens' New Court and of the Cam. Given the basically simple form of the architecture, its visual success relies on the proportions and materials. The full-height concrete columns of the structure are clad with Portland stone, while exposed edges of the floor slab are unclad white concrete. Transoms and mullions are of polished concrete, and window frames are bronze with the apron panels below faced in lead.

□

The Orchard 1899-1901

Shire Lane Chorleywood, Hertfordshire	190

architect **Charles Voysey**

Voysey built The Orchard for himself and it is an excellent example of his domestic work, though perhaps of more modest scale than the more famous Broadleys, Windermere (1898-9). The composition is basically symmetrical, but Voysey just slightly jars this perception by the off-centre door and the long, sweeping roof on the east side. Otherwise the façade is fairly plain: the regular spacing of the window bands further emphasises the near-symmetry. The inside is simple, with Voysey's own wallpaper used for decoration. But Voysey, unlike his contemporary in the United States, Frank Lloyd Wright, tended to avoid spatial experimentation inside his houses.

□

St Ann's Court 1936-7

St Ann's Hill Chertsey, Surrey	189

architect **Raymond McGrath**

An unusual round house, constructed of reinforced concrete, and set in picturesque eighteenth-century gardens originally laid out by Charles Hamilton. McGrath designed St Ann's for Christopher Tunnard, himself a landscape architect, and the curious form of the house is sliced like some great round of cheese, opening up to views down the hill and over the garden. The windows of the hall, study and dressing-room on the east side frame one magnificent cedar, and the living-room, dining-room and pools in the formal garden create an axis for a second cedar on the other side. Since McGrath did not like the effect of rendering concrete, rough Oregon boarding was used for vertical shuttering and the surface texture of the wood is retained.

□

Quarr Abbey 1908-12

off A3054
Fishbourne, Isle of Wight

192

architect

Paul Bellot

Bellot is one of the curious, unsung geniuses of twentieth-century architecture. Nikolaus Pevsner, in his Buildings of England, rightly puts Bellot in the Expressionist line of descent with Antoni Gaudi and Hendrik Petrus Berlage, but references to him in the standard literature are extremely rare. Bellot studied at the Ecole des Beaux Arts in Paris, but after receiving his diploma in 1900 he entered the monastic life in 1904. He built a number of buildings in Holland, Belgium, France and Canada, but Quarr, where he lived much of his life, is his masterwork. As with early Gaudi, the Dutch Expressionists and, most exceptionally, Fritz Höger's work, Bellot's Quarr Abbey, grows out of the inventive use of brick. The church, the most interesting building, is long and thin, with an almost square, low nave without aisles, succeeded by a long choir up a flight of steps, and closed by a square altar space. A turret with conical spire rises from the south-west corner of the choir, while the altar is topped by a square tower. The entire complex is of a mottled pink brick. Bellot's use of brick is most spectacular in the Moorish rib vaulting of the tower. The refectory, also by Bellot, is a broad hall with low pointed brick arches.

☐

Castle Drogo 1910-30

off A382, turn at Sandy Park
Drewsteignton, Devon

191

architect

Edwin Lutyens

Castle Drogo is one of the last grand, baronial English houses. Built on a magnificent site overlooking the gorge of the river Teign, the massive, picturesque massing of granite was originally intended to be more than twice as large. What remains, however, though rather stark and austere, contains some of Lutyens' most impressive spaces. The sloping site is used to advantage in the many changes of level throughout the castle, and it is in fact the grand staircase that stands out in the design. The granite walls are fully exposed in the staircase, which opens up to a series of domical vaults. Even when the granite is partly covered in the interior, with oak, painted panelling or plaster, it always makes its presence felt somewhere in the room. Among the other particularly inter-esting features of the castle is the basement kitchen, with furniture designed by Lutyens, topped by a large, cylindrical lantern. Castle Drogo is now a National Trust property.

☐

Glasgow School of Art 1896-9, 1906-9

Renfrew Street
Glasgow, Scotland

193

architect **Charles Rennie Mackintosh**

The Glasgow School of Art, Mackintosh's greatest work, was the result of a limited competition won by Honeyman and Keppie with a design by the young assistant Mackintosh. The constraints on the design were severe: a steeply sloping site and a meagre £14,000 budget. The board of governors stated, 'it is but a plain building that is required', and it is perhaps these constraints that produced the tension between a basically severe, dour structure and free-flowing decorative elements.

The front elevation is dominated by two ranges of giant, north-facing studio windows with the reinforced concrete lintels above exposed. Decorative ironwork, utilising the floral motif found throughout Mackintosh's work, springs up to the windows. (This ironwork also serves to help window-cleaners balance their ladders.) The asymmetry of the central entrance contrasts with the straightforward nature of the rest of the elevation. The western half of the school, with the three soaring, square-paned bay windows was built nearly ten years after the first half because of the limited budget. The bays provide natural light for the double-height library, and the imagery recalls a Scottish laird's medieval castle. After passing through the art nouveau entrance, one encounters the spectacular central staircase, which climbs up to a large, vaulted central space used for exhibitions. Mackintosh's decorative skill and spatial inventiveness is every-where evident: door windows, handles, balustrade carvings, iron-work, friezes on stairwells, all derive from the architect's hand. Mackintosh personally supervised each phase of construction and, as in most of his work, modified details as work proceeded in order to achieve the desired effect. Among the many interesting rooms is the director's office, just above the entrance, which was designed in 1906.

A dark-wood forest of right angles, with lights similar to contemporary work by Frank Lloyd Wright, the sheer durability of the library is one of the greatest testimonials to Mackintosh's design: for the School of Art has not become a museum where one can admire Mackintosh at a safe distance, but has remain-ed an active institution where Mackintosh chairs, doors and stairs are used intensively each day.

□

Willow Tearoom 1903-4

217 Sauchiehall Street
Glasgow, Scotland

194

architect **Charles Rennie Mackintosh**

The Willow Tearoom was one of a series of tearooms Mackintosh designed for Miss Cranston, but unfortunately it is the only one still remaining in any form. Mackintosh was responsible for absolutely every detail of the Willow Tearoom, except for the china, but today it is only the basic shell that survives. The plain cement façade, painted white, was a shocking declaration of modernity in its day, and even today, on drab Sauchiehall Street, its effect is startling. The ground floor is opened up with the grid of square-paned windows characteristic of Mackintosh. Above, a gently curving wall encases a long strip window. Inside, one can still gain some sense of Mackintosh's design. The main dining-room on the ground floor was decorated with the plaster frieze of abstract willow trees. From here, one can climb the open staircase, with its balustrade of steel, glass balls and wrought iron, which opens on to a balcony around three sides. Continuing upwards, the staircase leads to the first-floor Room de Luxe, a small, oval apartment painted white. Originally, the frieze of mirrors combined with the white high-backed Mackintosh chairs created a dream-like world far removed from the bustle of Glasgow.

□

Scotland Street School 1904

225 Scotland Street
Glasgow, Scotland

195

architect **Charles Rennie Mackintosh**

Mackintosh is best known for his works for what might be termed 'artistic' clients: Hill House for Walter Blackie ◇ 198, the Glasgow School of Art ◇ 193, the tearooms for Miss Cranston ◇ 194. But with the Scotland Street School, Mackintosh worked to a standard schoolboard budget and plan, yet managed to achieve some of his characteristic touches. The composition is symmetrical, with separate entrances for boys and girls (a small entrance in the centre is for infants). The street façade is dominated by the two semicircular stair-towers, almost entirely of glass with stone mullions. The blocks at either side of the main body of the school contain the diminutive cloakrooms. A few hints of Mackintosh's decorative urge can be seen in the stone carvings of the rear façade. The wrought-iron railing at the front is also characteristic of the architect.

□

Burrell Gallery 1972-83

Pollok Park, Pollokshaws Road
Glasgow, Scotland

196

architect **Barry Gasson**

The Burrell Gallery, built to house the extraordinary collection which businessman William Burrell donated to the city of Glasgow, is a pavilion in a park, similar in many ways to Bo & Wohlert's Louisiana Museum, Humleboek, Denmark (1958) ◇ 21. Visitors enter through the Romanesque sandstone portal from the sixteenth-century Hornby Castle: many of the architectural fragments from Burrell's collection have been integrated into the gallery building itself. The entrance is into a kirk-like wing that extends out from the main part of the gallery. From this entrance wing visitors pass through into an internal courtyard flooded by light from the glazed ceiling. Beyond this lie the main gallery rooms which press virtually into the surrounding woods so the path amongst the art works seems almost like a forest walk. The constantly reiterated motif of the pitched glazed roof is supported on concrete columns which carry the giant wooden rafters.

☐

St Mary the Virgin 1902-4

Great Warley, Essex

197

architect **Charles Harrison Townsend**

St Mary the Virgin, a memorial church built by Evelyn Heseltine to commemorate his brother, Arnold, seems a fairly conventional Essex church as one approaches through the Garden of Rest. The simple rendered rough-cast walls are capped by tiled gable roofs and a small timber belfry and spire rising above the west wall and its rose window. The Garden of Rest itself has a nearly symmetrical layout of gravel paths cutting through the close-cropped areas of grass. This external simplicity and restraint contrasts with the decorative richness revealed inside the church. Townsend was responsible for the joinery, as well as the actual building, but William Reynolds-Stephens designed all the other fittings, including font, screens, throne and lights. Heywood Sumner designed the stained glass, but unfortunately most of his work was lost in the war in 1940. What remains, however, is a grand composition defined by the foliage of the floral rood-screen. Six brass 'trees' support the screen, with angels perching atop the crown of each tree. The screens lead the composition to focus on the figure of Christ in the centre of the reredos, for the designers intended the Resurrection to be the central theme of the church. As in all the best works of the Arts and Crafts movement, much of the genius of the design of St Mary is in the decorative detail. In the brass stems of the rood-screen foliage, for example, are glass pomegranates and mother-of-pearl flowers.

☐

Hill House 1902-3

architect **Charles Rennie Mackintosh**

8 Upper Colquhoun Street
Helensburgh, Strathclyde

198

Hill House, built for the publisher Walter Blackie, is the built version of Mackintosh's 1901 project Haus Eines Kunstfreundes. The form of the house is decidedly Scottish: stone walls covered with rough-cast (harling) for the structure, and long gabled roofs and small windows. But Mackintosh's mark can clearly be seen in the almost abstract composition of the outside, the windows punched through the grey walls, the characteristic bay bulging out on one side. The effect is achieved not through decoration, as inside, but through the massing of the various parts. Mackintosh is responsible for every detail inside the house: the design of the carpets, cabinets, furniture, light fittings, bath and shower fittings, etc. Fortunately, the house is now run by the National Trust for Scotland and most of the interior and its fittings is very well preserved.

From the entrance, everything is cloaked in dark-stained oak, with the exception of a few light stencils or tiles. The grand main staircase is revealed through an open timber screen. Off the main hall are the library (now used as an information centre) and the magnificent white drawing-room. On axis with the entrance to the drawing-room is a bay window and window-seat framed by flower-like columns. The walls are stencilled with a silver geometric pattern, highlighted with floral patterns in pink and green. A steel-framed fireplace sits in one corner of the room surrounded by a floral mosaic inlay. The gesso plaster panel above the mantelpiece is by Margaret Macdonald Mackintosh, the architect's wife. The other grand room of the house (though they are all worth study) is the white bedroom. L-shaped, like the drawing-room, with a low-arched ceiling that creates a formal alcove over the bed and its associated closets.

☐

Home Place 1903-5

architect **Edward Schroder Prior**

Cromer Road
Holt, Norfolk

199

The grand Home Place, now a convalescent home, was built for the Reverend Percy R. Lloyd and cost a vast £60,000. On one level, Home Place is an almost wild exercise in the use of local materials: Pevsner calls Prior's passion for local materials 'fanaticism'. The walls are of solid concrete faced with pebbles found on site, thin tile-like bricks, and bonded-in cut stone. The whole is arranged in a pot-pourri of local patterns: windows are connected vertically by St Andrew's crosses, ground-floor windows are set in brown stone, parapets are of brick slates, the tall chimney-shafts are paired square piers and St Peter's columns. This wild composition conceals the symmetrical plan and elevation (historian Hill Franklin has termed this type of plan a 'butterfly plan'). Some of Prior's effects have been spoiled by unfortunate modifications to the house: the garden façade, the most extreme of Prior's composition, is distorted by a modern porch and standard metal window frames have replaced many of Prior's casement windows.

☐

Downs Road
Hunstanton, Norfolk

200

architect

Peter and Alison Smithson

The rigidly symmetrical steel structure of the Smithson's school heralded the return of Modernism to Britain after the war years. Although it is often credited as marking the beginning of British Brutalism, that judgement seems a bit harsh. The inspiration for the school is Mies van der Rohe, rather than Le Corbusier, and Mies' dictum that 'God is in the details' has been carried to an almost obsessive extreme. The Smithsons won the commission for the school as the result of a competition, and their scheme is carried out with what some call viciousness, although before weathering there was undoubted elegance. Everything has been stripped and refined: a structure of steel with infill panels of yellow brick or glass, and everything exposed on the interior as well as the exterior. The original buildings are grouped around a two-storeyed hall, with a single-storey dining-room opening off. The classroom blocks are two storeys, distributed around inner courtyards. Because of increasing numbers of students, numerous later buildings have been constructed. The water tower with its three X panels was perhaps the school's most heroic statement, but it has now been lined with concrete because of constant rusting.

Heathcote 1906

architect **Edwin Lutyens**

King's Road
Ilkley, Yorkshire

201

With Heathcote, Lutyens changed his style from quasi-Arts and Crafts to Classical. He claimed at the time that Classicism was essential to set the house apart from the 'villadom' of the surrounding suburbs. The result is characteristically Mannerist Classicism and rather severely grand. The symmetrical composition has a recessed central bay with a tall, pantiled hipped roof. This three-storey central element is flanked by two-storey projecting wings, topped by pyramid roofs. The entrance façade is comparatively subdued, but Lutyens' plastic inventiveness with Classical motifs is brilliantly displayed on the garden façade. Lutyens primarily uses the Doric, with half-columns framing the ground-floor windows in the wings and a standard triglyph and metope frieze

running above. The composition builds inwards to the centre, but the use of Classical decoration fades as the central bay is neared. As is often the case with Lutyens, the treatment of windows on each floor is different: recessed rectangular windows on the ground floor, circular and round-arched windows on the first floor and tiny square attic windows. Smooth quoins are used throughout to define volumes and contrast with the textured ashlar.

☐

Impington village college 1936-8

architect **Gropius and Fry**

Impington, Cambridgeshire

202

Gropius and Fry worked together for two years, between Gropius' arrival from Germany and his departure for the United States. The best of the works completed in that time, the Impington village college, was originally a school for Henry Morris's progressive community and educational programme. The village colleges were intended as regional centres for social and cultural needs, containing classrooms, clinics, libraries and institutes in one complex. At Impington, a central building houses the concourse, cloakrooms, etc., and provides the pivot for the wings that contain the other activities: the classroom wing leads off at a right angle, the 'adult wing' (common-room, sports-room and library) is at right angles in the opposite direction. At the end of the

concourse, the wedge-shaped hall projects out into the grounds. The college has red-brick buttress walls, and is faced with yellow brick, blue tiles and scarlet ironwork. More recent additions, which have somewhat spoilt the original effect, are by the county architects' department.

☐

Princes Street
Ipswich, Suffolk

203

architect **Foster Associates**

The chutzpah, the bravura it takes to build a completely glass wall down to the pavement on a busy street, with no protection, is visible throughout Foster Associates' headquarters for Willis Faber Dumas, a large insurance company. Foster's architecture is wrapped up in immaculate details, stunningly smooth surfaces and technological marvels. No other work of his, with the possible exception of the Sainsbury Centre for the Visual Arts ◇ 244, displays these three characteristics so superbly. The exterior of Willis Faber is a sinuous curtain wall of glass with no mullions, no real hint of what is holding up the glass. During the day, the black glass reflects its surroundings which are for the most part unattractive, but the curve (the shape is vaguely reminiscent of a grand piano) distorts shapes and images into abstracts, hiding the banality of the building's neighbours. At night, the curtain wall disappears, and Willis Faber reveals its inside offices, mechanical plant and all the frills of a luxurious headquarters.

As often happens with a smooth-surfaced work, the entrance is not well defined, but once inside the best part of Willis Faber is revealed. Foster has created a grand ceremonial 'staircase' of escalators running up the centre of the building, constantly filling the work with motion and life. The interior details — balustrades, ceilings, lighting — are all made with the same precision and smoothness as an exterior. Yet there is something chilling about all this smooth perfection. Everything has been so carefully executed, so beautifully finished, that it is hard to actually 'engage' the building. Willis Faber has a 'don't touch' atmosphere that makes it a work more to be admired than enjoyed. The other sour note in Willis Faber is the typical, deep open-plan office space. Because of fire regulations and ventilation requirements, no one actually sits by all those windows. With the circulation corridor on the outer edge, most workers are condemned to a rather gloomy existence. In good weather, however, they can escape at lunch-time to the roof-top garden. This greensward for lounging and recreation is the one light, humorous touch in a serious and impressive, High-Tech wonder. □

Kings Walden Bury 1971

near Hitchin, Hertfordshire **204**

architect **Erith and Terry**

Erith & Terry persevered in the Classical style for years when it invoked the ridicule of the architectural profession. Their unusually well-heeled clients, however, welcomed the chance to have newly built Classical buildings, and with the turn of the wheel in the late seventies, Quinlan Terry (following the death of Erith) found himself courted by architectural magazines round the world. Kings Walden Bury is perhaps the best example of their country-house style: a sort of attenuated neo-Georgian, with overtones of the Baroque. The grand pedimented entrance porch uses correct superimposition of the orders, with Doric columns on the ground floor and Ionic columns above. Although Classical columns can be ordered from catalogues, made out of

glass-reinforced plastic and other new materials, Erith & Terry built their works out of traditional materials.

□

Engineering Faculty 1959-63

Victoria Park
Leicester **205**

architect **Stirling and Gowan**

The engineering building for Leicester University is in some ways the herald of the British High-Tech of the seventies. The concrete structure is clad in the characteristic red brick of Stirling and Gowan, industrial glazing is unashamedly exposed and inside nothing is hidden. As influential as this matter-of-fact treatment of the machine age was the plastic handling of the volumes of the building, which are expressed in an almost Constructivist manner: lecture-halls are wedge shaped (recalling Melnikov), classrooms have full-height glazing, the spiral staircase is wrapped in a cylinder of glass, laboratories have slit-like windows, and the workshops are like an advanced industrial shed. The roof-lit workshops occupy most of the site, which was the architects' original

justification for the tower. A very high proportion of the tower block is taken up by the circulation space: stairs, lifts, corridors: with the actual classrooms being rather small. Although the ingenuity of the plan is remarkable, it seems perverse that every floor, despite the similar accommodation, has a different plan. The design's obsession with form at the expense of other considerations has led to considerable problems: the building has weathered badly, glazing has had to be changed to prevent damp penetration, and the glazed classrooms have proved to be sweat-boxes in summer (and an almost impossible environment for computer screens because of the glare, but this could not have been anticipated).

□

Horniman Museum 1896-1901

100 London Road
London SE23

206

architect **Charles Harrison Townsend**

The Horniman Museum, one of the most eccentric products of the Arts and Crafts movement, was built to house the anthropological collections of F. J. Horniman MP, a rich tea-merchant. The long, thin museum is anchored at one corner by the free-form tower which contains the entrance. Starting square in plan, the tower slowly grows upwards into a circle, with four cylindrical, foliated columns poking into the sky. The steps to the grand voussoired Romanesque doorway are on axis with the grand mosaic panel by Robert Anning Bell, of the Art Workers' Guild, before they turn to lead into the museum. The free-flowing forms of the exterior are belied by the interior which had a fairly straightforward plan. Townsend's original plan, badly altered now, started on the balcony of the south gallery, from where visitors moved on to the ground floor of the north gallery (the museum is on a sloping site). Stairs between the galleries lead to the ground floor of the south gallery. High barrel vaults with roof-lights lend ample natural light. The few foliated decorations Townsend executed inside have horrifyingly been plastered now.
☐

Whitechapel Art Gallery 1899-1901

80 Whitechapel High Street
London E1

207

architect **Charles Harrison Townsend**

The Whitechapel Art Gallery, which opened in the same year as Townsend's Horniman Museum ◇ 206, shares many characteristics with the larger work in south London. The basically symmetrical façade is jolted by the off-centre entrance: a completely out-of-scale voussoired Romanesque doorway. Townsend originally intended that the towers be capped by cupolas and the panel between them filled with a mosaic, but the gallery trustees ran out of money before this could be completed. The interior was cleverly arranged with a narrow first-floor hall, allowing natural light from the roof-lights down the sides of the ground-floor hall.
☐

Sanderson's factory 1902-3

Barley Mow Passage
London W4

208

architect **Charles Voysey**

The factory for Sanderson's, the wallpaper manufacturers, is one of the few industrial buildings by an Arts and Crafts architect. Given the cottage-industry philosophy of the movement, this is unsurprising, but Voysey's factory is unabashedly 'industrial' in appearance. Large piers of white and blue glazed brick provide the structure for the big small-paned windows with white spandrels. Segmental arches of the windows and the languid droop of the gable-like parapets, however, suggest the more free-flowing style of the Arts and Crafts.
☐

Houses 1904

38-9 Cheyne Walk
London SW3

209

architect **Charles Robert Ashbee**

Ashbee, one of the leading architects of the Arts and Crafts movement, designed eight houses on Cheyne Walk, but unfortunately only two now remain. The houses are designed to blend in with what were once the surrounding Georgian dwellings, in red brick and with simple proportions. But Ashbee elaborated this standard form with his free-flowing stylistic elements. Of the two remaining houses, 39 is fairly humdrum, but 38, which was originally an artist's house and studio, is dominated by a large, white-rendered asymmetrical gable. The studio, behind this gable, was lit from the rectangular windows as well as by the swivelling porthole window in the middle of the gable. The asymmetry of the gable matches the lines of the house with the differing height of the neighbouring buildings. The street railings, reminiscent of Mackintosh's work, with their ornamental gold balls, were probably made at Ashbee's Guild of Handicraft.
☐

Michelin House 1905-11

architect
F. Espinasse

91 Fulham Road
London SW3

210

Michelin House is one of London's oddest buildings, a strange combination of art nouveau and completely idiosyncratic design. Its closest companion, at least for the ingenuity of decoration, is New York's Chrysler Building, though the small scale of Espinasse's work makes it far more quirky. Built at a time when the automobile was still a curiosity, Michelin House is a celebration of motoring and, particularly, tyres. Tyres crop up in the unlikeliest places: bulging out of structural piers, as decoration in pediment friezes, as gable ends.

☐

The Black Friar 1905

architect
H. Fuller Clark

174 Queen Victoria Street
London EC4

211

In the ground floor of a fairly ordinary Victorian office block, Fuller Clark designed one of the best surviving Arts and Crafts interiors in London. The exterior offers only a few hints of the richness within: the mosaic tympanum and the carved entablatures brimming with beasts and devils. The saloon bar and snack bar, in the vaults beneath the railway, are the richest parts of the interior. The saloon bar is dominated by the large inglenook, marked by a low tripartite arch. Bronze reliefs, by the sculptor Henry Poole, march frieze-like around the room. The snack bar is even more exuberant: a three-bay barrel vault of gold, white and black mosaic arches overhead, while more of Poole's bronze reliefs adorn the walls. Side walls are further enlivened by six alabaster capitals illustrated with nursery rhymes and sixteen smaller capitals with quirky little animals.

☐

Hampstead Garden Suburb 1906

architect

Parker and Unwin

London NW11

212

Hampstead Garden Suburb resulted from the energies of Dame Henrietta Barnett and the notions of garden suburbs (Bedford Park, Chiswick) and garden cities (Letchworth, Hertfordshire). The original trust purchased 128 hectares of land on the west fringe of the Hampstead Heath extension on both sides of Hampstead Way and Wellgarth Road, which is the identifiable garden suburb. The intention was that this would be an area for a mixture of classes to live with access to essential amenities and facilities to improve the mind and spirit. Hence, smaller houses for the working class, housing for single working ladies (Waterlow Court by Baillie Scott ◇ 214), housing for the aged, churches and the suburb's institute for education are all included. The Central Square, with its public buildings, is placed on the highest ground, dominating the suburb and

providing a focus for the rest of the plan. Streets are a combination of gentle curves and short straight stretches, with streets for traffic and purely residential streets clearly distinguished. All houses have private gardens and are divided from one another by hedges rather than by walls. The density throughout the suburb is only twenty houses to the hectare.

Hampstead Garden Suburb was immensely influential both in Britain and abroad, and many of its individual buildings are of considerable excellence. But as is immediately apparent today, the original ideal of a mixture of classes has broken down. The low densities have meant that public transport was uneconomic and therefore nonexistent, the rarefied atmosphere of Central Square has been a barrier to shops and other services. □

St Jude and Parsonage Institute 1908-10

Central Square
London NW11

213

architect

Edwin Lutyens

In the midst of Parker and Unwin's picturesque plan for the garden suburb, Lutyens devised a formal town centre that combines elements of both town and country. The Institute occupies the most important position, closing the main axis of the design with its courtyard. Of grey bricks with red dressings and stone trim, the Institute is one of the most successful examples of the Wrenaissance style that characterises many of Lutyens' early public buildings. The two churches are similar in style, but St Jude is probably the more interesting. The enormous roof starts virtually from the ground, and covers the three-bay tunnel-vaulted nave and aisles. Even the gable end of the nave is partially swallowed by this roof. Only tall dormer windows and the tall spire break through this blanket covering. Inside, the tunnel vault of the nave collides with the dome vault of the crossing. Arches and piers are of red brick, but this Classicism is contrasted by open timber lean-to roofs in the aisles. □

Holland House 1914

1-4 and 32 Bury Street
London EC3

215

architect

Hendrik Petrus Berlage

Holland House is one of the few works in Britain by any prominent foreign architect. Berlage, the great Dutch architect of his day and the forerunner of the Amsterdam School and the Expressionists, received the commission from Helen Kröller-Müller, a great patron of art. Holland House has an awkward L-shaped site, snaking around existing buildings. Hence there are two entrances to this vertically composed work. Tall windows lie between the structural steel mullions, which are clad with green-glazed tiles. The plinth and angle strips are of black granite. Particularly interesting is Joseph Mendes da Costa's prow-like granite sculpture on the south corner. Inside, the entrance halls are richly decorated with glass mosaic, and the steel beams are left exposed and painted black. A refurbishment of the interior in 1983 hid much of Berlage's interior, particularly the tiled staircases and toilets, but the entrance halls were cleaned, revealing Berlage's inventive decoration.
□

Waterlow Court 1909

Heath Close
London NW11

214

architect

M. H. Baillie Scott

Baillie Scott, a vigorous defender of the Arts and Crafts until his death in 1945, designed numerous multiple housing groups for Parker and Unwin's Hampstead Garden Suburb, but Waterlow Court was the only one ever built. Originally designed to contain fifty flats for single working women, it was one of the first and most successful examples of housing for single persons. Waterlow Court is approached through a timber-covered passage which opens into the two-storey cloistered courtyard. The central pavilion is topped by a bellcote, suggesting the rather utopian rural vision of Baillie Scott. The gardens are reached through the corners of the court.
□

Midland Bank headquarters 1924-39

Poultry/Princes Street
London EC3

216

architect **Edwin Lutyens**

Lutyens is justly best known for his country houses, but he was a prolific commercial architect, building banks, steel-framed office buildings, hotels, etc. The Midland Bank headquarters is his largest work in England and one of the most accomplished in his idiosyncratic Classical style. The double-height base is heavily rusticated with round-arched windows and a Tuscan order entrance. Above this is a frieze-like mezzanine storey, above which are three storeys grouped together by tall arches with mild rustication. The stone blocks of the rustication gradually diminish in height and almost imperceptibly step back as the building rises. Egyptian-style obelisks mark the corners of this three-storey bay, and an aedicule, in a rough Palladian window form, grandly marks the centre. The aedicule is crowned by a low dome, set back in line with the top two storeys of the building. The ground-floor banking hall, of green and white marble, is one of London's grandest.

☐

Battersea Power Station 1929-55

architect **Giles Gilbert Scott**

Nine Elms Lane
London SW8

217

The massive 'temple of power', the Battersea Power Station, is one of the major industrial landmarks of London, but, no longer operational, its future is in doubt. Built in two sections (1929-35 and 1944-55), its distinctive exterior was the responsibility of Scott, who was called in to alter the 'pedestrian brick elevations' of the engineers. Appropriately, the bulk of Scott's work was in church design (he won the competition for Liverpool Cathedral in 1903, when he was only twenty-three years old). The corners of the enormous structure are defined by towers capped by the tall fluted-column chimneys. Scott had originally designed red square-section chimneys, but the final result makes the station look vaguely like a four-legged table turned upside down. The interiors are equally impressive and of gargantuan scale. The turbine hall, which no longer has its humming machines, is decorated and lined in marble, like some Roman baths for Titans.

☐

Hay's Wharf and St Olave House 1931-2

Tooley Street
London SE1

218

architect
H. S. Goodhart-Rendel

Hay's Wharf and its adjoining office building are one of London's rare examples of <u>Moderne</u> architecture. The triangular-sectioned wooden letters that announce the name immediately fix the date of the building, but there are other interesting features. To allow easy access to the river, the entire building stands on bronze-clad columns, while the bulkhead windows allow ample natural light into the offices (particularly important on narrow Tooley Street). The centre panel of the river façade is outlined with a black granite frame and panels of gilded faience designed by Frank Dobson. Directors' offices and the boardroom lie behind. The mosaics on the Tooley Street front are by Colin Gill. The interior is chock-full of <u>Moderne</u> decoration, equalling the better-known <u>Daily Express</u> building.
☐

Daily Express building 1932

Fleet Street
London EC4

219

architect
Owen Williams

From the outside, the <u>Daily Express</u> building is one of London's finest Modern works: slick black glass panels flush with transparent glazing, all cleanly delineated by chromium strips. Inside the entrance hall, one finds the supreme art deco interior of London with metal relief sculptures exalting the Empire. The lighting is in the 'stalactites' suspended from the ceiling. Some idea of the innovation and bravura behind the design can be judged by the roughly contemporary neo-Greek banality of the <u>Daily Telegraph</u> building (Elcock & Sutcliffe, with Thomas Tait, 1928). Williams, the great architect-engineer of his generation, designed the <u>Daily Express</u> Manchester office as well.
☐

Hoover factory 1932-5

architect
Wallis Gilbert and Partners

Western Avenue
London W5

220

A grand, <u>Moderne</u> celebration of a factory, the brilliant colours of the Hoover factory proclaim the dignity and modernity of the company, the importance of its calling. In the finest art deco tradition, the façade is vaguely Classical, with its temple-like front made memorable by the grand starburst entrance. The scalloped corner windows to the end towers, however, are a far more Modernist device. The other parts of the factory, though not so rich in decoration as the Western Avenue elevation, are a good example of thirties, cleanly designed, Modern architecture.

☐

Arnos Grove underground station 1932-3

Bowes Road/Arnos Road
London N11

221

architect
Charles Holden

Underground stations seem often to inspire excellent architecture: Guimard in Paris ◇ 78 and Wagner in Vienna are perhaps the most notable examples. But London Transport, in its heyday in the twenties and thirties, was also responsible for some fine buildings, notably Holden's work on the Piccadilly Line stations (Holden also designed London Transport's headquarters, 1927-9).

Arnos Grove is typical of the work, and, because of its resonance with other buildings, particularly interesting. Holden's stations are invariably marked by some tall feature, in this case the cylindrical drum of the booking hall. Simple geometries are the rule, and decoration is stripped to a minimum. Inside, Holden was innovative in his use of uplighting, notably in the escalator shafts. Arnos Grove, with its cylinder above a square base, bears a striking formal resemblance to Asplund's City Library, Stockholm (1920-8) ◇ 290, and Ledoux's Barrière de la Villette (1784-89).

☐

Royal Institute of British Architects 1932-4

65 Portland Place
London W1

222

architect

Grey Wornum

The Scandinavian Classicism of Wornum's RIBA headquarters won a competition in the early thirties: a sign of how influential architects like Asplund and Tengbom were at the time. A large box of a building clad in Portland stone, the most interesting aspect of the exterior is the grand entrance, with its ceremonial bronze door and large triple-height window above. Free-standing pillars flank the entrance, and are topped with statues by James Woodford (this overt modern Classicism must have been an embarrassment to members for decades until the revival of interest in historic styles in the seventies). The interior, though impressive, is not so well planned, for the vast bulk of the space seems to be taken up with circulation space rather than useful, and much needed, rooms. Perhaps the most notable feature of the building is that it contains one of the world's finest architectural libraries, open to the public.

□

Isokon flats 1933-4

Lawn Road
London NW3

223

architect

Wells Coates

The Isokon flats look rather sorry and worn today, but when built they heralded the arrival of Modern movement architecture in London. The large unbroken surfaces of white-stuccoed concrete in a geometric composition of heavy horizontal balcony parapets against the diagonals of the external staircases are the basic vocabulary of twenties Modernism on the Continent. The flats were built for Jack Pritchard, whose Isokon Laminated Furniture company produced the avant-garde designs of Marcel Breuer. Pritchard intended that the flats be a collective of units for single professionals, and the design included a bar and clubroom. In its early years, Lawn Road was in fact the home of the English Modern movement and the associated artists, writers and poets. Breuer lived there when he came as a refugee from Germany, and Pritchard provided Walter and Ise Gropius with a flat when they, too, arrived in London.

□

Penguin pool 1934-5

London Zoo
London NW1

224

architect
Lubetkin and Tecton

The penguin pool is certainly the most loved and best-known work of Modern architecture in Britain. The narrow spiral ramps of reinforced concrete were the result of the architects' studies which revealed that the penguins would be encouraged by the shape to promenade and form orderly queues. The plan of the pool is oval, in contrast to the loose spirals. The floor surfaces are of a variety of materials, slate, rubber and bare concrete, in the belief that the agitation of the penguins' feet would help relieve their boredom. Despite its evident visual success and sculptural mastery, the penguin pool does have problems, the most serious being the rendered screen walls which block children's view.
☐

Pioneer Health Centre 1934-5

St Mary's Road
London SE15

225

architect
Owen Williams

The Pioneer Health Centre arose from the social experimentation of Drs Scott Williams and Innes Pearse, who believed that preventative health care was the answer to society's ills. Peckham was chosen as the site of the experiment because, at the time, the area contained a good mixture of social classes. The centre includes medical clinics as well as a gymnasium, swimming pool, theatre, cafés and other ancillary spaces. Owen Williams, who trained as an engineer, designed a structure based on a standard reinforced concrete column of minimal cruciform shape. Circular bays are cantilevered out above these, terminating in flower-boxes and iron railings. The swimming pool is at the centre of the plan, and at the flanks are two double-height spaces: a gymnasium at one end and a theatre/lecture hall at the other. The ground floor is left open on one side to provide a covered children's playground. Above this, on the first floor, is the lounge, with full-height sliding windows overlooking the grounds, and a glazed wall overlooking the swimming pool on the other. Views through the entire building can be had because of the glazed wall opposite on the first-floor café. The second floor contains the medical rooms as well as the library and study areas. The roof, designed to be used as a playground, has a sinuous railing that curves inwards to eliminate the danger of children climbing up and falling over.
□

Simpson's department store 1935

203 Piccadilly
London W1

226

architect
Joseph Emberton

The strip windows, clearly expressed structure and the roof canopy, declare the progressive style of Simpson's a pioneering work in Britain. The welded steel structure was devised by Felix Samuely, who had been responsible for the De La Warr Pavilion, Bexhill-on-Sea, the year before ◇ 183. Emberton was particularly successful in the exterior lighting of Simpson's, which reveals the influence of art deco even though the building itself is more purely Modern. The internal planning of the store was also innovative, with a series of rooms substituting for the normal vast, open space. Luxurious materials, again resonating with art deco touches, are used throughout. The top two storeys, which mar the exterior, were added in 1963 by the Architects' Co-Partnership.
□

Sun House 1935

architect
Maxwell Fry

9 Frognal Way
London NW3

227

The Sun House is one of the best Modern movement houses in Britain, and one of the few that compares with contemporary and earlier work on the Continent. On a steeply sloping site, the ground floor is reserved for the garage and boiler-room (reminiscent of Le Corbusier's minimal ground floors) and the retaining wall. The main rooms of the house, therefore, are gathered at the front, taking advantage of the views with their bands of strip windows. A balcony terrace runs the length of the first floor, supported on remarkably thin steel columns. At the eastern end of this terrace, the balcony bursts forward over the garage, to provide a covered entrance to the house. On the second floor, the main bedroom-bathroom suite opens on to a small terrace. The structure is of concrete, and the smoothed external surface is painted white.

☐

Highpoint 1 and 2 1936, 1938

North Hill
London N6

228

architect
Lubetkin and Tecton

Highpoint 1, upon its completion, became the symbol of Le Corbusier's Modern architecture in Britain, but just two years later Highpoint 2 was the focus of howls of dissent from the faithful. Le Corbusier's five points of modern architecture are well-illustrated in both works: pilotis, free plan, strip windows, roof garden and a free façade. The plan of Highpoint 1 is a double cruciform with eight flats on each floor. The structure is of reinforced concrete, and except for some brick on the ground floor, is white-rendered. Curved balcony parapets connected by thin iron bars to the walls (and necessitating hidden structural contortions) give the work the true imprint of the thirties. In the design of Highpoint 2, Lubetkin had to respond to the loud protests of local inhabitants to the undisguised modernity of the first block. So the concrete is hidden with brick and tile cladding and, most memorably, two reproduction casts of the Erechtheum caryatids support the entrance porch instead of the Modern unadorned round columns of Highpoint 1. Yet in completely depriving his caryatids of any context, Lubetkin has the last laugh at his critics who felt Highpoint 1 lacked historical references.

☐

Pine Street
London EC1

229

architect

Lubetkin and Tecton

The tiny Finsbury Health Centre is the last of the series of Modern movement works by Lubetkin and Tecton in the thirties. The concept of the health centre, pioneered in Peckham Pioneer Health Centre (1934-6) ◇ 225, was itself progressive so it is apt that the architecture of both these centres was at the forefront of British design. The building has a two-storey H-plan, with the simple rectilinear wings spreading out from the complex main block at the centre. The centre is approached up an inclined concrete ramp which crosses a moat before the main doors. Glass blocks make up the entire ground-floor façade, clearly encased in the bulging concrete frame. The first floor has a large roof terrace overlooking the entrance area, while on the roof the lecture-hall bursts out of the building's confines.

□

Royal Festival Hall 1951

South Bank Arts Centre
London SE1

230

architect

LCC Architects Department

The 1951 Festival of Britain on the South Bank was the grand celebration to mark the end of the deprivation of the war and post-war years. Architecturally, it also marked the public unveiling of the curiously spindly British version of the Modern movement. The Royal Festival Hall, with its 2,600-seat concert hall, was the only permanent building of the festival. Under the influence of Le Corbusier, the architects of the London County Council designed a concrete box which breaks open to reveal its various parts: the concert hall itself bursting out above, and the public spaces visible through the large glazed front wall (the Festival Hall is in fact one of London's few modern buildings that does not turn its back on the Thames). The interior is a perfectly preserved 1950s design, with the curvaceous boxes in the hall and cantilevered staircases in the lobbies. In 1962, the Festival Hall was extended and recased, much to the detriment of the original design.
□

Barbican 1959-81

architect

Chamberlin Powell and Bon

London Wall / Aldersgate
London EC2

231

The Barbican, a complex of 2,113 flats and an arts and conference centre, is built on an area of the City that was devastated in the war. The notion was to provide housing for those that had to or wanted to live close to the centre of the City. The architecture, in keeping with the prevailing aesthetic of the years in which it was designed, is comprised of massive concrete structures: 125-metre-high housing towers, slab-block housing and the central arts complex which is largely buried in the ground. Unfortunately, by the time this architectural monolith was well underway, public opinion had sensibly rejected the notion of large, walled-off ghettos for either housing or the arts. Although some of the elements of the Barbican are good examples of their type (the theatre, the home of the Royal Shakespeare Company, is very successful), the entire complex ranks as one of the largest white elephants in central London.
□

National Theatre 1967-77

South Bank Arts Complex
London SE1

232

architect **Denys Lasdun & Partners**

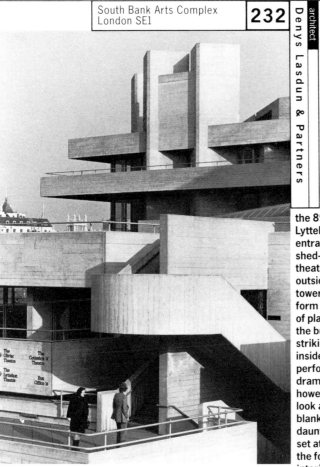

The National Theatre sits at one end of the South Bank Arts Complex, with the Royal Festival Hall at the other. Everything in between is the worst sort of sixties concrete Brutalism. But Lasdun's National Theatre is, despite its faults, one of the few buildings of the sixties or seventies in London that anyone should be encouraged to see. It is, in fact, a complex of three theatres, the 1,160-seat Olivier with an open stage, the 890-seat proscenium Lyttelton, and, with its own side entrance, the 200- to 400-seat shed-like Cottesloe. The two main theatres are expressed from the outside by the tall concrete fly-towers, while cantilevered terraces form a strongly horizontal series of planes around the river side of the building. At night, the effect is striking, with the crowds of people inside milling about before a performance and the structure dramatically lit. During the day, however, the concrete tends to look a bit forbidding (the vast, blank concrete rear is particularly daunting). Because the Olivier is set at 45 degrees to the Lyttelton, the foyers are an exciting, lively interior space, with terraces and stairs cutting through the high spaces. The relative success of these foyers, which undeniably have a sense of 'theatre' about them, can be judged by comparing the concrete foyers of the Barbican Arts Centre, which is more akin to an airport than a theatre or concert hall.

☐

Robin Hood Lane housing 1968-72

architect **Alison and Peter Smithson**

Robin Hood Lane
London E14

233

Robin Hood Lane is by no means the worst of the now largely discredited huge, concrete housing estates of the sixties and seventies, but its interest lies in the enormous influence the Smithsons had in those years. For Robin Hood Lane is the realisation of the Smithsons' much-broadcast urban polemic, which began with their project for Golden Lane in 1953. Two long slabs of pre-cast concrete surround a central park dominated by a large artificial mound. The site is cut off from its admittedly dreary surroundings by large concrete walls and moats. The housing is characterised by the Smithsons' famous 'streets in the air', which have proved ripe settings for vandalism and violence.

☐

Alexandra Road housing 1969-79

architect
Camden Architects Dept.

Alexandra Road
London NW8

234

Alexandra Road marks the end of the era of comprehensive housing re-development. An enormous crescent of concrete houses, intended as a modern interpretation of the Victorian terrace, the complex includes housing for 1,660 persons in 520 units, a training centre for mentally handi-capped children, a childrens' reception centre (closed because the building was found to be unsuitable), a school and a park. The main terrace backs on to the main line railway with a giant eight-storey wall largely screening out the sound of the trains. The housing is mostly south-facing, with the internal planning devised so most rooms use the terraces and catch the sun (kitchens and toilets overlook the railway). Pedestrian pave-ments are isolated from roads, which run below the main level of housing to reach the garages. Together with other contemporary works by the Camden architects, Alexandra Road is one of the most accomplished housing estates of the seventies, but by the time of its completion its gigantism had largely gone out of favour with architects and public alike.

☐

Own house 1975

architect
Michael Hopkins

49a Downshire Hill
London NW3

235

The Hopkins house, built on a steeply sloping site, is one of the most successful of glass and steel box houses, surprisingly blending in unobtrusively with the traditional architecture of the rest of the street. The house is entered at first floor by a metal bridge. Both street and garden sides are totally glazed, with only venetian blinds offering privacy for the inhabitants (the luxuriant weeping willow at the entrance also offers a cloak of privacy). The flanks of the house, in contrast, are of stove-enamelled corrugated metal sheet. One of the few domestic works of the British High-Tech architects, the house is derivative of the famous Eames house, Santa Monica (1949) and the California Case Study houses of the fifties.

☐

Houses 1976-80

11-13 Elstree Hill
Lewisham, London

236

architect **Segal and Broome**

This relatively ordinary-looking group of houses is of interest more because of the process than the design of the architecture, for they are examples of timber-frame self-build houses built by families with no building experience. Segal and Broome acted as consultant architects to the families, who followed Segal's plans and specifications. Lewisham Borough Council provided the funding and the sites (difficult sites which would have been untenable for conventional public housing) and arranged the random draw in which interested families on the council's housing waiting-lists could participate in the scheme. Segal's plans were intended for the self-builder: flat roofs, all timber construction, houses lifted off the ground (eliminating the need for levelling of site), and no load-bearing walls. The result, a kind of modern half-timber style, is a self-builder's vernacular.
□

Lloyd's 1981-6

107 Leadenhall Street
London EC3

237

architect **Richard Rogers & Partners**

The new Lloyd's building, home of the famous insurance exchange, is London's analogue of the Centre Pompidou in Paris by Piano and Rogers ◇ 99. But where the Pompidou is an exercise in beautifully detailed steel structure, Lloyd's is devoted to an exploration of the limits of reinforced concrete. To maximise the unobstructed interior space, the main structural elements and the services (lifts, staircases, main vertical risers for air ducts and cables) are pulled to the outside of the building in a series of towers. The interior is dominated by the massive ground-floor Room, the actual exchange hall, and the central atrium which rises the height of the building.
□

TV-am 1983

Hawley Crescent London NW1	238	architect **Terry Farrell Partnership**

In a disused garage on a back street, TV-am marks a revival of twenties jazziness in architecture: art deco mixed with Busby Berkeley. The curving front screen wall, which sweeps the eye around the crescent, is dominated by the oversized keystone with its blue neon lighting. The rather scrappy entrance court seems a disappointment after this opening, but the main lobby recaptures the glitter of the keystone. A ceremonial ziggurat staircase stands in the middle of the lobby, from which gangplanks give access to both sides of the _piano nobile_ first-floor newsroom. The canalside elevation is a colourful blue, yellow and red, with glass-fibre eggcups in place of a Venetian palazzo's pineapples. ☐

First Church of Christ, Scientist 1903-8

Daisy Bank, Victoria Park Manchester	239	architect **Edgar Wood**

The bizarre amalgam of forms in Wood's church is a cross between the Arts and Crafts and what would later be termed Expressionism. One approaches the church on the central axis and confronts the white-rendered brick façade, topped by the central stone chimney-stack. Below this chimney lies a long round-headed window with two-light windows extending to the left and right to create a cross. The round-arched Romanesque portal is built out of cut bricks. Ranged symmetrically around this unconventional entrance are two wings, projecting diagonally from the centre. To the left is the reading room which, on both sides, has a canted bay window. At the junction of the hall and the church itself stands a stubby round tower with a conical roof. The composition of the whole seems to have been piecemeal, accumulated over the ages because of this curiously placed tower. The building is now a community centre named after the architect. ☐

Milton Keynes shopping centre 1979

Midsummer Boulevard
Milton Keynes, Bucks.

240

architect
Milton Keynes Architects

The shopping centre in Milton Keynes is, as much as anything can be, the heart of this most ambitious of new towns. In the first half of the twentieth century, as for centuries before, the core of a town (such as Hampstead Garden Suburb) was a church or the town hall. But in Milton Keynes, commerce reigns supreme. The shopping centre is a finely detailed Miesian block nearly 700 metres long consisting of three parallel bands of shopping accommodation. Since Milton Keynes is a city entirely dependent on the automobile, the centre has been designed to maximise the amount of car parking available within easy walking distance: 5,500 cars can be parked within four minutes walk through a series of steel <u>porte cochères.</u> The three bands of shopping in the centre are served and separated by two 12-metre-wide, 14-metre-high enclosed, naturally lit pedestrian arcades. Between these arcades, the central band contains the main shops and two public squares, one open and one covered. As elsewhere in Milton Keynes, pedestrians and vehicles are strictly segregated: a raised access road at first-floor level allows deliveries to be made throughout the day to the shops.
□

Centre for Advanced Study 1969-71

architect
Edward Cullinan

Minster Lovell, Oxfordshire

241

The study centre at Minster Lovell is a brilliant contemporary exercise in Cotswolds vernacular, so subtly done that it is at times hard to distinguish between the new and old buildings. Cullinan started with a group of three existing buildings, an L-shaped house, an oblong garage (once a malt house) and a small T-shaped barn. The house was converted into a reception area, dining-room, kitchen and offices, the garage into a library, and the barn into conference rooms. Along the gravel path between the house and the barn stretches the new block of study-bedrooms which shelters an internal stone-flagged path between the house and barn. The broken roofs, stepped ridges, splayed eaves and gables of the complex combine with the traditional materials (Cotswold stone and timber) to integrate seamlessly with the village vernacular. Among the many details which respond so sensitively to the surrounding landscape is the grass-topped bridge which almost invisibly crosses the river opposite the cloistered stone-flagged path. The Centre for Advanced Study makes an interesting comparison with MacCormac Jamieson & Pritchard's Sainsbury Building, Worcester College, Oxford, of a decade later ◇ 247.
□

Byker
Newcastle-upon-Tyne

242

architect
Ralph Erskine

Byker, both visually and in terms of the process of design, marks a crucial break with the mainstream of post-war housing re-development. Planners had decided to replace the existing run-down Victorian terraced houses, partly because of a planned motorway that would have cut through the area creating large noise problems (the motorway has never been built).

Erskine's design responds to the particular problems of the site, but it is more specifically an attempt to preserve the community spirit of old Byker and to incorporate the wishes of the residents in the new housing. A large perimeter block of housing, known as the Byker Wall, lines what was to be the motorway side of the site, varying in height with the contours of the land: at three points in its undulating path it reaches eight storeys, but mostly it is five storeys and at some points only three storeys high. Behind this perimeter block lies mostly low-rise housing woven together with a series of pedestrian routes and communal landscaped areas. But this bare description conceals the true richness of the Byker design. In order to rehouse 9,500 residents without disrupting family ties and the traditions of the neighbourhood, Erskine decided to make his design more participatory than imposed: an architect's surgery in a former undertaker's shop was set up to explain designs, to offer advice and guidance (the surgery remained open for years after completion) and to take

suggestions from the residents. A pilot scheme of forty-six dwellings was built at Janet Square as a test design, and the residents' responses to this first stage were incorporated in later stages. The details of the architecture itself are appropriately eclectic and varied: the almost overwhelming exterior of the Wall (without the logic of a roaring motoway next to it) is a kilometre-long mural in four contrasting colours of brick, while the more open inner side has timber decks stained red, green, blue and brown. The low-rise housing also uses a wide range of colours and materials. Bright, strident colours of stained timber are often overlaid on more sober brick structures. Timber slats are a constant motif, often arranged in rhythmic patterns that echo various details. The lush land-scaping has meant that Byker seems to grow better with the passing years, rather than deteriorate like most of the housing of the sixties and seventies. □

Inmos factory 1982

architect **Richard Rogers & Partners**

Cardiff Road
Newport, Gwent

243

The gleaming, High-Tech Inmos factory is an interesting elaboration of the suspended structure of Rogers' Fleetguard warehouse, Quimper (1981) ◇ 103. The simplicity of Fleetguard is transformed at Inmos into a structure of beguiling visual complexity: the basic principles can be grasped visually, but the proliferation of cables and ties suggests there is more to the structural analysis than is first apparent. The building is organised in a series of bays, with a central service spine. The spine provides the main circulation corridor, and above, the structure of the spine supports the bulk of the services required for the large 'clean room' where the assembly of microchips takes place. The attention devoted to the bright-blue, nautical-looking structure by the

architects and engineers has left the actual building envelope slightly neglected: the 'clean room' half of the building is identified by the blank, grey aluminium cladding-panels, while the offices and laboratories in the other half have a random chequerboard of blank and glazed panels.

□

University of East Anglia
Norwich, Norfolk

244

architect **Foster Associates**

The Sainsbury Centre is the ultimate slick, smooth, High-Tech shed, an aircraft hangar for fine art. The structure consists of thirty-seven welded tubular prismatic steel trusses spanning 35 metres, supported on lattice towers to create a column-free interior 133 metres long. Within this shell, two independent mezzanines are inserted. The structure is clad with three types of panels, glass, solid and grilled, which can supposedly be interchanged by undoing six bolts. In practice, however, the cladding seems to have remained static. The panels themselves were a significant technical innovation, being of sandwich construction with a moulded outer skin of anodised aluminium; individual panels are sealed with neoprene gaskets which also act as rainwater channels. At the two ends of the tube of the building are clear glass walls, 30 metres across and 7.5 metres high, supported by 7.5-metre high glass fins. These glass walls give views out to the lake to the east and the woods to the north: fortunately, the centre turns its back on the dreadful concrete ziggurat of Denys Lasdun's University of East Anglia. The centre is spectacularly entered via a glass bridge that pierces through the north side at upper level; visitors then reach ground level inside down a spiral staircase. The centre includes two exhibition galleries, the university's school of fine arts, a restaurant, library, basement storage and workshop facilities, and an entrance conservatory.

□

St Catherine's College 1964-6

architect

Arne Jacobsen

Manor Road
Oxford

245

A strictly mathematical composition in the most refined Modern style, St Catherine's College stands as a monument to an architectural movement and as an example of that movement's manifest shortcomings. The main group of buildings consists of two long linear blocks of student accommodation which define a central quadrangle. A T-shaped building with senior common-rooms and junior common-rooms on the two wings and the dining-hall at the base of the T stands at the head of the quadrangle; a circular lawn then separates this block from the paired rectangles of a library and lecture block. All of the structures are of prefabricated reinforced concrete. Although the buildings are well detailed, they lack any of the atmosphere and happenstance of the older colleges at Oxford. Jacobsen's design could as easily serve as a corporate headquarters or an industrial complex as a college. The one lyrical touch is the 180-metre-long water garden that runs along the entrance side of the college and creates the same symbolic separation of college and town as the heavy medieval towers, walls and gates of Oxford's more ancient buildings.

□

Sir Thomas White Building 1975

architect

Arup Associates

St John's College
Oxford

246

The Sir Thomas White Building is an elaboration, and in many ways a refinement, of the Cripps Building by Powell & Moya at St John's College, Cambridge (1967) ◇ 188 . A precast concrete skeletal frame is clearly expressed as a series of pavilions alternating with service towers. Within this skeletal frame lies a secondary enclosure of glazing, and within that lie the actual rooms with their softer materials: maple floors, woollen rugs, hessian wall-surfaces. The building is a rough L-shape around a courtyard (the angle of the wings is 85 degrees rather than 90 degrees so that an existing tree could be spared). The pavilions are four-storey groupings of four rooms, lavatory, shower and small kitchen on each floor.

□

Sainsbury Building 1980-3

architect **MacCormac and Jamieson**

Worcester College
Oxford

247

The Sainsbury Building, a student hostel that serves as conference accommodation during university vacations, is one of the best examples of the continuing vernacular strain in British architecture in the seventies and eighties. In the picturesque setting of Worcester College's eighteenth-century gardens, it blends unobtrusively and creates a continuation of the college's architectural virtues. At first sight, the Sainsbury Building appears to achieve this solely through a sensitive adherence to surroundings: a warm yellow stone that blends with old college walls, a low, stepped form to close off the view across the lake. But seen more closely, the complexity of the building reveals itself, for MacCormac and Jamieson are adherents of what has become

known as the Cambridge School: an architecture based on meticulously calculated grids and geometries. The new paths created by the building echo the older patterns of college walks, but the composition of the whole is at times more reminiscent of M. C. Escher than Capability Brown, particularly in the steps that take one down to the lakeside common-room.

□

Landfall 1937-8

architect **Oliver Hill**

19 Crichel Mount Road
Parkstone, Poole, Dorset

248

Hill is among the more interesting British architects of the thirties, for in an almost nineteenth-century manner he switched his style to suit his client, programme or mood. But Landfall is one of his best Modern movement houses. The client, Dudley Shaw Ashton, had discussions with Eric Mendelsohn, Berthold Lubetkin and Wells Coates before deciding on Hill, and Hill rose to the challenge of such competition. Landfall is long and narrow, designed to retain the existing pine trees on the site. A curving white garden wall with steel lettering announces the house. The entrance front is mostly solid, with only the curved wall of the staircase-bay pierced by portholes. Towards the garden, however, the house opens up. The circular hall lies between the dining-room and living-room,

and the three can all open into one large, flowing room. These rooms have sliding glass doors that open on to the Pompeian red terrace. Above, the bedrooms open on to a continuous balcony and a glazed-in sunroom and open terrace are on the roof. The main walls of the house are of cavity-brick construction, rendered and whitewashed externally. The elegantly curving external stair leading from the balcony to the terrace is, however, of reinforced concrete.

□

Portmeirion 1926-59

off A487
Gwynedd, Wales

249

architect **Clough Williams-Ellis**

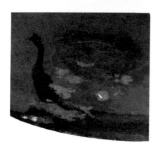

Portmeirion can either be seen as one of the grand follies of the twentieth century, or as a brilliantly sustained polemic against the sterility of much of twentieth-century architecture (although the two roles are not entirely incompatible). Changing architectural tastes this century have led to the prominence at various times of both views, but in the seventies, with the growing interest in Historicism and Revivalism, Portmeirion became one of the touchstones for a large number of architects. A small 'village' on a peninsula of North Wales, Portmeirion is entirely the expression and invention of Clough Williams-Ellis. It was probably best described by Christopher Hussey in Country Life in 1930: 'This fantastic acropolis is an architect's dream fulfilled – a glorious medley of Italy, Wales, a pirate's lair, Cornwall, baroque, reason and romance.' Williams-Ellis himself described it at times as a 'Home for Fallen Buildings'. For Portmeirion is a picturesque agglomeration of a wide variety of different architectural styles, grouped into an almost surrealist village (it achieved fame in the sixties as the setting for the strange television series, The Prisoner). The village is made up both of buildings and bits of buildings that Williams-Ellis bought elsewhere (the Jacobean ceiling in the Town Hall's Hall of Hercules, for example, he bought at auction for £13 since no one else wanted it) and new works.
□

St Andrew 1906-7

Roker, Sunderland
County Durham

250

architect **Prior and Wells**

The tall tower of St Andrew, a landmark for boats at sea, seems at first glance to mark a fairly typical neo-Gothic church. But close examination reveals one of the most original, and successful, of twentieth-century churches. Rough grey local stone further suggests the ordinary nature of the church, but in the Gothic-shaped windows arches are done away with: straight lines prevail throughout. The tower, too, is slightly out of kilter, for it stands over the chancel yet the east end of the chancel projects slightly beyond the tower, creating a gable end. Inside more surprises await. The large nave is articulated by the wide parabolic stone arches, carried on short double shafts. The arches are of concrete reinforced with iron rods, while the ridge and purlins are of concrete reinforced with steel. Only the rafters are wooden, which is quite unusual in a work of the Arts and Crafts. The shape of the nave suggests, according to Pevsner, the upturned keel of a boat. The relative plainness of the church is contrasted by the rich furnishings: a Burne-Jones tapestry for the reredos, the chancel carpet to a William Morris design, altar cross, candlesticks and the processional cross by Ernest Gimson, the stone font by Wells and the dedication plates and foundation stones by the young Eric Gill.
□

Sonning, Berkshire

251

architect

Edwin Lutyens

Deanery Garden, perhaps the best example of Lutyens' Romantic vernacular style, was built for Edward Hudson, the founder of <u>Country Life</u>. The house, of red Berkshire brick, is built around three sides of a courtyard, with the fourth side closed by an ancient brick wall. The central gateway leads down one side of the court through a vaulted passage to the front door. All the axes of the house, including this entrance route, extend out to the gardens, designed by Gertrude Jekyll. The vaulted passageway to the entrance is also broken midway to allow entrance to the court with its central fountain, or, in the other direction, one of the subsidiary axes of the garden. The main garden/entrance axis lies to the side of the main axis of the house, which is marked by the large oriel window overlooking the garden, the large hearth (an echo of Frank Lloyd Wright's contemporary work) and the statue in the courtyard. The soft, red brickwork sits under a large tiled roof. The brick walls are plastered internally, but in the main double-height hall, the ashlar of the entrance passage is used as infill between the oak bracing. The stair, with its open joists and expressed dowels, is typical of Lutyens' work at this time and displays his debt to the Arts and Crafts.

Library 1911

architect **Ernest Gimson**

Bedales School, Church Road
Steep, Petersfield, Hampshire | **252**

Gimson is well known as one of the
leading furniture designers of the Arts
and Crafts. His last work, the library
and hall at Bedales School, is a fine
example of neo-Tudor, especially
inside. Gimson's building is connected
to the slightly earlier main building (by
E. P. Warren, 1907) by a timbered
passageway. The brick exterior, with
leaded casements, is conventional, but
the massive timber roofs inside are far
more interesting. The library has a
double-height central reading-area,
with stacks on ground floor and
gallery. The great roughly hewn timber beams
rise steeply to form the open timber roof.
□

Renault parts distribution centre 1982-3

architect **Foster Associates**

Rivermead Estate
Swindon, Wiltshire | **253**

An interesting comparison
can be made between
Foster's Renault distribution
centre and Rogers'
Fleetguard factory, Quimper
◇ 103, both completed
around the same time. Both
are suspended structures,
with the roof supported by a
circus-tentlike system of
columns and rods in
tension. But whereas Rogers
chose a visually simple
structure, which is basically
rectilinear in appearance,
Foster's structure has an
almost Baroque richness (justified
by the architects on the grounds
that the structure is more
efficient). What is particularly
interesting about this distinction is
that Foster is traditionally the
refined Classicist of High-Tech
architecture, whereas Rogers,
particularly in the Centre
Pompidou, Paris, has the
reputation of being the exuberant
Romantic of High-Tech. Perhaps
these two works mark a change in
position. Aside from the bright
yellow structure, magnificently
detailed as always with Foster, the
most interesting aspect of Renault
is the vast, overscaled porte
cochère at the entrance end.
□

Nashdom 1905-9

Taplow, Buckinghamshire

254

architect **Edwin Lutyens**

Nashdom is Lutyens' finest exercise in his distinctive neo-Georgian, the style that dominated the middle years of his career. In characteristic Lutyens' fashion, the architecture of the house is in part a pun on the name, for Nashdom can almost be seen as updated and slightly out of kilter John Nash. The design is surprisingly simple, with the almost unadorned whitewashed brickwork contrasted by the green shutters on the south side. The north entrance front of Nashdom is slightly awkward, as the house steps down with the steep slope of the site. A Tuscan loggia connects the two seemingly disparate parts of the house, behind which is an apsidal court. The south, garden front is the more successful part of the exterior. The green and white contrast creates a very domestic, nearly urban feel, but Lutyens disturbs the equilibrium of the design by almost retreating from the centre: the nearly symmetrical wings of Nashdom meet in a central composition of a lowered cornice and absence of shutters. Behind this curiously recessive centre lies the double-height, top-lit winter garden.

□

St Mary's 1908-30

Knox Road, Wellingborough Northamptonshire

255

architect **Ninian Comper**

Comper was the best and the most original of those church architects who persisted in revivalist design in the twentieth century. He started his career with George F. Bodley, one of the great architects of the Gothic revival, but by the time of his masterpiece, St Mary's, a number of other influences had altered his style. After a trip to Italy and the Mediterranean in 1904, Comper began to synthesise a wide variety of historic styles in his work. The exterior of St Mary's is a rather stern English Perpendicular in ironstone. Inside, however, the continuous fan-vaulting is carried on octagonal pillars with capitals decorated with lilies. Byzantine majestas are suspended from the vault, while the baldacchino is Italianate and the screens combine Greek, Italian, Spanish and English detail: the rood-screen, for example, has gilded and painted Tuscan columns and a Gothic loft and rood. Comper said of St Mary's, 'Only to its contemporaries does the church owe nothing.'

□

Concrete House 1934-5

4 Ridgeway
Westbury-on-Trym, Bristol, Avon | **256**

Connell, Ward & Lucas

With Tecton, Connell, Ward & Lucas were the principal purveyors of Modern movement architecture in Britain in the thirties. Amyas Connell's 1929 High and Over, Amersham ◇ 180, was probably the first of the Modernist houses in Britain, but the Concrete House is the first to use Le Corbusier's 'Dom-ino' structure of reinforced concrete, with the grid of columns allowing all internal partitions to be non-structural. The entrance porch, with its curving, free shape stands independent of the main structural framework. The glass staircase rises above the roof of this porch and is supported on steel columns. The south façade of the house, the entrance front, is almost entirely glazed with continuous plate-glass windows.
□

the Faber GUIDE

to twentieth-century ARCHITECTURE

The Netherlands

267

257-265   266

272-273

276-277

268-271

274   275

Exchange 1897-1903

architect

Hendrik Petrus Berlage

257 Beursplein 1·3
Amsterdam

Berlage won the international competition for the Amsterdam Exchange in 1897 against a field that included the great Viennese architect Otto Wagner. Berlage's masterpiece, which is frequently credited as the first Modern building in the Netherlands, is clearly a Dutch work: the red bricks, the vaguely medieval look of the flat walls punctuated by thin windows, and the rich stone-carving. The Exchange, although far more restrained than what was to come, was the touchstone for the principal architects of the Amsterdam School, De Klerk, Kramer and van der Mey. The Exchange is an enormous building, particularly within the relatively small-scale context of Amsterdam. Over 140 metres in length and 55 metres in breadth at its widest, it houses stock, grain and produce exchanges as well as numerous ancillary facilities. The wide variety of spaces inside the building is expressed externally both through the fenestration and the outlines. Although relatively traditional in appearance, the Exchange's design was actually based on a rational, geometric system inspired by the great French nineteenth-century architect Viollet-le-Duc. The plan is based on the square, while the elevations derive from a grid of isosceles triangles with a ratio of base to height of 8:5. Overlaid on this rational design are rich decorative touches. Berlage collaborated with a number of artists, including Mendes da Costa, for the relief sculptures and J. H. Toorop for the mosaics. The large open exchange halls, topped by glass roofs supported by thin metal trusses, are the richest parts of the interior. Polychromatic brick patterns vie with the predominantly yellow surfaces.

American Hotel 1902

architect

Willem Kromhout

258 Leidseplein 28
Amsterdam

The American Hotel is an extraordinary amalgam of art nouveau, Islamic and High Victorian details. Kromhout's work shares many traits with the exactly contemporary Exchange by Berlage ◇ 257: an 'honest' expression of structure, decorative use of brick. But Kromhout's pale-buff bricks and literally fantastic decorative structure stand in distinct contrast to the sober, dark brick of Berlage. Both exterior and interior details recall the art nouveau, particularly when the date of the design is considered, but Kromhout's decoration has none of the curvilinear, naturalistic character of the art nouveau. Instead his decoration, especially his use of bricks, is semi-abstract and rectilinear.

□

Scheepvaarthuis 1912-16

architect

Johan Melchior van der Mey

259 Prins Hendrikkade 108-114
Amsterdam

The headquarters office for the shipping companies is the first and most extreme work of the Amsterdam School Expressionists. The Scheepvaarthuis is constructed of reinforced concrete, but its exuberant, elaborate brick cladding with terracotta and concrete ornament creates its striking impression. This decoration has no particular relation to the structure, but crescendos to a climax in the fantastic roofscape, clearly visible from Amsterdam's harbour. Van der Mey was responsible for the basic form of the exterior, but the actual sculptures of the exterior were by a group of artists: W. C. Brouwer, H. A. van den Eijnde and H. Krop. The decorations of course relate to shipping and the sea. Symbolic figures of the Atlantic and Indian Oceans flank the main entrance, while all around the building, even on the service entrance, are sculptures of ropes, cables, signs of the zodiac and other nautical emblems. The rich decoration is continued in the public areas of the interior. The design for the glass roof in the main hall is by yet another artist, W. Bogtman. Some of the furniture for the building was designed by De Klerk.

□

Eigen Haard housing estate 1913-20

architect

Michel de Klerk

260 Zaanstraat
Amsterdam

De Klerk's Eigen Haard housing estate, built in three separate phases, is the greatest work of the Amsterdam School. Although the Scheepvaarthuis ◇ 259 holds the distinction of being the first work of the school, it was the Eigen Haard that truly set the style and became an example for housing in particular both in Holland and abroad. Although the first block on the Spaarndammerplantsoen is the least interesting of the Eigen Haard works, De Klerk had already formulated the essence of the style: taut planes of brick are enlivened through occasional explosions of especially shaped and coloured brick for decorative use, unusually shaped windows framed in white-painted sash are flush with the wall plane. Part of the Amsterdam School's particular character is given by the undersized local brick used in all of their buildings, which adds a richness to the wall texture not obtainable with normal-sized brick. In the first Eigen Haard estate these elements are handled fairly conservatively, with only the parabolic gables hinting at the extraordinary shapes to come. The second Eigen Haard estate shows De Klerk's considerable extension of the decorative uses of brick. The taut, almost unbroken wall plane of the first estate is here continuously interrupted: a triangular bulge for one entrance, a semi-circular bay shielding another. Bricks are laid vertically and obliquely, as well as horizontally, and De Klerk's use of polychromatic patterns is

extensive: red, yellow, purple and black bricks are used as are black and red tiles.

The perimeter block of the third estate has 103 housing units in addition to a post office and separate meeting hall. De Klerk's invention reached its peak in the third estate: towers and turrets, curves and bulges burst out of the wall plane everywhere. The barrel-like oriel windows jut out of the flats like captain's quarters on an old sailing ship. De Klerk's invention was not purely wilful, however, for it grew in part out of a conviction that workers should not be condemned to identical, anonymous flats (De Klerk himself was from a working-class family). The extreme of De Klerk's play with forms is in the post office that occupies the corner of the site. One critic has likened it to 'a child's toy enlarged to architectural scale in some contemporary setting for Diaghilev's Ballet Russe', but seen from the right angle it seems to be a giant steam locomotive pulling the line of housing behind it.

☐

architect

Kramer and Michel de Klerk

261 P. L. Takstraat
Amsterdam

The De Dageraad housing estate is the climax of the work of the Amsterdam School. What had started in 1912 with the Scheepvaarthuis would, after De Dageraad, virtually die out as De Klerk and Kramer, the two leading exponents, became more and more restrained and tame in their buildings. There are already signs of this growing restraint in De Dageraad, but because of the outburst of virtuosity from Kramer, this housing estate remains with the Eigen Haard ◇ 260 the best example of the Amsterdam School.

Kramer is responsible for P. L. Takstraat 1-25 and 2-26, Burgemeester Tellegenstraat 14-36 and 38-60, Therese Schwartzeplein 1-13 and Henriette Ronnerplein 2-14. His best work, however, is on P. L. Takstraat (shown here). Buff and brown bricks are swept into waves of curves, with the breakers crashing on the street intersections. The three-storey ranges of flats along the street are relatively straightforward, but the sweep of the form and the stepping back of the façade clearly define each unit, giving a sense of identity on a street of similar buildings. At the street intersection with Burgemeester Tellegenstraat, however, the buildings step suddenly up to five storeys, with a central chimney-tower yet taller embraced by tiers of brick curves. De Klerk designed Therese Schwartzeplein 15-33, Henriette Ronnerplein 16-34 and P. L. Takstraat 27-31 and 28-32. On P. L. Takstraat, De Klerk's contribution seems unnecessarily sober when contrasted with the exuberance of Kramer's curves.

□

Nederlandse Handelmaatschappij 1926

architect
K. P. C. de Bazel

262 Vijzelstraat 30-34
Amsterdam

De Bazel's massive building for the Nederlandse Handelmaatschappij is a rare Dutch variation on a more typical North American building type of the twentieth century: the headquarters office building meant to impress and humble by sheer scale and weight. The structure here is of concrete clad in granite. De Bazel was an Amsterdam architect who toiled steadily in the shadows of a series of greater architects, but his best works have a solidity and strength that recalls Berlage. Of particular interest in this work are the almost primitivist sculptural decorations that spring out of the granite bands: the monster guarding the safe deposit is by De Bazel himself. ☐

Open-air school 1929-30

architect
Johannes Duiker

263 Cliostraat 36-40
Amsterdam

A constant preoccupation with twentieth-century architects has been the interplay of indoors and outdoors, and perhaps no single building has so thoroughly explored this contrast as Duiker's Open-air school. Of reinforced concrete construction, the four-storey cube has been sliced open on its south corner to create a series of open terraces. The enclosed parts of the cube have the folding glass windows clearly distinct from the concrete columns, which are set back. The educational philosophy which inspired Duiker's design held strongly to the belief that children, in order to be healthy, have to have fresh air and plenty of natural light (a similar philosophy to the Montessori schools nearby ◇ 264). So the design imposes virtually no barrier between children and the outdoors. The open terraces, in fact, become a series of outdoor 'rooms' of equal stature to the indoor rooms. The ground-floor wing to the south-east is the gymnasium. The staircase climbs up the middle of the cube. Among the many interesting details of the Open-air school is the heating, which is in the ceiling panels of each of the seven classrooms and the gymnasium. ☐

Montessori school 1935

architect
Willem van Tijen

264 A.Durerstraat 36
Amsterdam

The Montessori school makes an interesting comparison with Duiker's nearby Open-air school of 1930 ◇ 263. A similar philosophy is behind the Montessori school — the need for natural light and fresh air — but the rather spindly steel and glass construction (which was partly chosen for rapid building) gives a far lighter feel than the concrete of Duiker's school. Again, as with Duiker's work, there is minimal separation between the children's classrooms and the outdoor recreation areas both visually and in terms of access.
□

Mothers' House 1978

architect
Aldo van Eyck

265 Plantage Middenlaan 33
Amsterdam

Aldo van Eyck is among the more important polemical figures in the architecture of the second half of the twentieth century. In the fifties, in both writings and design, he broke away from the prevailing functionalism to seek architectural inspiration in other sources: children and primitivism. His activities have tried to assert the home as the spiritual core of life, and man at the centre of the home. His interest in children and imaginative activity is reflected in the over 600 playgrounds van Eyck has designed. The Mothers' House is a characteristic outgrowth of these interests. Van Eyck's Mothers' House is a temporary refuge for single mothers and their children, and it is this social programme that provides the building's design rationale. The bright colours of the Mothers' House — blue, red, yellow, orange and green — emphasise that this is a place for children and warmth, while the structure itself combines a contradictory image: both open and welcoming and closed and private. The façade is a response to the nineteenth-century eclecticism of the street in this quiet area of Amsterdam. The steel and glass of van Eyck's work offers a sense of transparency that the heavier early buildings do not possess, but the Mothers' House wraps comfortably around the old. The entrance is actually through one of the nineteenth-century buildings.
The modern five-storey building along the street is broken asymmetrically to offer a secondary entrance and to provide views through the glazed stair-tower to the courtyard beyond. A low wing runs out to the courtyard. The front part has a structure of concrete columns and slabs with claddings in steel.
□

Centraal Beheer office building 1973

architect	
Hermann Hertzberger	
266	Prins Willem Alexanderlaan 651 Apeldoorn

Centraal Beheer is beyond doubt one of the seminal office buildings of the twentieth century. In many ways it represents the extreme of workers' democracy in their environment as even a quick visit to the interior will demonstrate. Part of the irony of this, and a principal reason for the success of Centraal Beheer, is that this democratic environment is encased in a rigid, precise shell that offers little hint of the individuality one finds inside. In a sense, Hertzberger's Centraal Beheer is like an Italian hill town: composed of identical elements all piled one on top of the other, yet containing multitudinous signs of individual expression once one penetrates the façade.

While Hertzberger's architecture provides the proper shell for Centraal Beheer, its interior is as much a product of the management as the architect. Each group of sixteen workers shares a work 'island' clearly defined by Hertzberger's rabbit-hutch plan. These islands typically overlook an atrium or common space, but each individual is free to decorate (or not to decorate) his or her area in whatever fashion is desired. Thus a ventilator grill becomes a focus for the grinning mouth of a mad mask, ferns droop all over, posters brighten some areas, while other areas are more sober. Circulation is via banks of open escalators that shoot across central atria, while throughout common areas exhibit the same invention as individual workplaces: a coffee area is kitted up like an Italian bar in one place. Small alcoves with comfortable chairs are scattered about for informal discussions, or quiet reading. What links these disparate improvisations is the rigid grid of the building. In a supposedly flexible typical office building, with large, undifferentiated deep floors, such a policy would produce visual anarchy. It is the very inflexibility of Hertzberger's architecture that allows such freedom.

☐

Park Meerwijk 1916-18

architect	
M. Kropholler and others	
267	Meerweg/Studler van Surchlaan Bergen Binnen (near Alkmaar)

The seventeen houses of Park Meerwijk are one of the most extraordinary collections of free-form, Expressionist architecture remaining. Perhaps the closest comparisons are the Steiner colony at Dornach, near Basel, and the later work by Bernhard Hoetger in Worpswede, Germany ◇ 156. But the Dutch buildings lack the rather eerie feeling of the Swiss and German Expressionist works: the warmer, more natural use of materials (brick, thatch and weather-boarding) accounts for the more inviting nature of the Dutch works. Throughout Park Meerwijk, however, houses have a literal connection with nature, for this is truly organic architecture. House walls extend to become staircases or garden walls, or sink into the earth. Among the most interesting of the individual houses at Park Meerwijk are the semidetached Meezennest and Merelhuis houses by Kropholler at one end of the central axis, with the central twin chimneys emphasising the symmetry of a decidedly picturesque-looking design.

☐

Leuring house 1903

architect

Henry van de Velde

268 | 30 Wagenaarweg
The Hague

Van de Velde studied painting at the Beaux-Arts Academy in Antwerp, the city of his birth, and this fine arts training is clearly visible in the Leuring house. Although part of the art nouveau movement (Jugendstil in the Germanic countries where van de Velde did a considerable amount of work), the Leuring house already shows some of the heavy, organic feel of van de Velde's work that was later to be an influence on the Expressionists. The sober, almost drooping appearance of the exterior, however, gives way to a richly decorated interior, still well preserved. The entrance hall is double height, with a double wooden staircase climbing the back wall and framing a magnificent art nouveau mural by van de Velde.

De Bijenkorf department store 1924-6

architect

Pieter Lodewijk Kramer

269 | Grote Marktstraat/Wagenstraat
The Hague

Kramer is best known for his work at the De Dageraad housing estate in Amsterdam and his many bridges, but the De Bijenkorf department store is one of his most interesting buildings. The use of brick in plastic curved surfaces, learned in De Dageraad ◇ 261, and in work on the Scheepvaarthuis with J. M. van der May ◇ 259, reappears on a grand scale in the corners and skyline of De Bijenkorf. The massive bays of leaded glass give the building a slightly medieval character, perhaps a retort to the growing band of Modern architects in Holland who were looking to Berlin and Paris for inspiration rather than to the Amsterdam School.
□

First Church of Christ, Scientist 1925-6

architect

Berlage and Zwart

270 | 1 Andries Bickerweg
The Hague

Although at first glance, Berlage's style seems to have changed little between the Amsterdam Exchange (1897-1903) ◇ 257 and his Christian Scientist church, in fact his use of brick has become far more dynamic, influenced perhaps by the younger architects of the Amsterdam School. Berlage's church has none of the free forms of the Amsterdam School, but his use of the brick wall to create and to reflect the spaces of his building owes a debt to the younger architects. The church is rigidly symmetrical, but the angular forms create a series of visual collisions of the exterior elements. The taut composition of Berlage's early works has given way in this later period to a much looser design where the various parts, rather than being knit together, are each separate and clearly defined. Piet Zwart was responsible for the interior of the church.
□

De Volharding building (now Randstad) 1928

architect

Buys and Lürsen

271 Grote Markt
The Hague

Originally built for the De Volharding co-operative society, this building on a major street is one of the few large-scale works in De Stijl in Holland. The striking profile of the building with its ascending composition of rectangular shapes recalls the early work of De Stijl, but the more conventional strips of windows on the upper floors are a visible reminder of the later date of De Volharding. One of the further marks of the twenties is the extensive use of glass blocks in the central stair-tower and the first floor: the classic use of the glass block in the Maison de Verre in Paris ◇ 91 is exactly contemporary with De Volharding.
□

Zonnestraal sanatorium 1926-8

architect

Duiker and Bijvoet

272 Loosdrechtsebosje 7
Hilversum

The Zonnestraal sanatorium was one of the most advanced early works of the Modern movement and it proved vastly influential: Aalto's Paimio sanatorium ◇ 42, for example, is partly modelled on it. As with the later Open-air school in Amsterdam ◇ 263, Duiker and Bijvoet used reinforced concrete to create a structure that opened the building up to natural light and fresh air. The plain white elements of the sanatorium are grouped symmetrically around a central services block. In contrast to the basic symmetry of the composition, the central block is animated by a bold, almost picturesque expression of elements.
□

City hall 1928-30

architect

Willem M. Dudok

273 Dudokpark
Hilversum

Willem Dudok trained not as an architect, but as a military engineer. But in 1915, he was appointed director of public works in Hilversum and, as part of his duties, was involved in the design of schools, public baths, an abattoir and sports facilities. Dudok is best known, however, for the city hall, which is justly regarded as one of the great works of the De Stijl movement in architecture. In the careful use of brick throughout the work, Dudok's indebtedness to the architecture of the Amsterdam School is revealed as well.

The city hall is arranged around a square courtyard, with projecting one-storey wings spreading in various directions. The main offices are on the ground floor, with the public rooms on the first floor. The regular geometry of the exterior is continued in the interior in both decoration and fittings. Properly proud of their great building, the city of Hilversum has carefully preserved the Dudok interiors.

Dudok's particular skill was in the balancing of horizontal and vertical elements, clearly seen in the exterior of the city hall. The horizontal character of the work is stressed by the long, thin buff-coloured bricks. This is offset by the tall clock tower on the southeast corner, which also serves as a water tower.

□

Housing estate 1924-7

architect

J. J. P. Oud

274 Scheepvaartstraat
Hook of Holland

Oud was the leading Dutch architect of the International style, and, with Mies van der Rohe, Gropius and Le Corbusier, was a pioneer in the development of Modern movement architecture. Oud crucially rose to fame with his work in and around Rotterdam, for his rise paralleled the rise of the almost antithetical Amsterdam School. Although initially influenced by the artists of De Stijl, particularly in his now-destroyed Café De Unie of 1924, the housing in Hook of Holland marks an important break by him from De Stijl. The two terraces of two-storey houses with shops at their ends spurned the use of colour, except for small highlights of primary colours on some minor wood and metal details. The smooth white-rendered walls and planar strip windows are archetypal marks of the early Modern movement, but Oud adds a touch of Romantic spirit to this Classical severity with the curved corners and the drooping lip of the cantilevered slab. Supposedly Oud's introduction of curves in this work infuriated and disgusted the still-loyal De Stijl artists.

☐

Van Nelle factory 1926-30

architect

Brinkman and van der Vlugt

275 Van Nelleweg 1
Rotterdam

The van Nelle factory is one of the triumphs of the early years of the International style: a complex of production, administrative and recreational facilities all brought together into a seamless, elegant whole. The design derives from the rationalisation of the production phases combined with the social belief in the integration of all activities related to the factory on one site. Hence the complex is basically composed of four blocks: a curved one for offices, and then blocks of eight, five and three storeys for the processing respectively of tobacco, coffee and tea. Warehouses, heating and electrical plant, sports hall and fields complete the site. The curving office block (which perhaps is a reminder of Dutch Expressionism) stands at the entrance to the site, sweeping the eye toward the 220-metre-long factory. Brinkman and van der Vlugt designed tubular-steel furniture and a variety of special fittings for the office block. A glazed bridge at first-floor level leads from the offices to the first factory block. A stair-tower and set of lifts at the intersection of the bridge and factory leads up to the circular tearoom with panoramic views over Rotterdam and the Dutch countryside. The layout of the three factory blocks follows the layout of the assembly lines, allowing complete mechanisation of the transport of materials throughout the factory. Raw material is transported by conveyor belt from the warehouses to the top floors of the appropriate factory block and then drops from floor to floor and is processed, sorted and packed. Elevated ramps take the finished products to shipping areas before they are distributed. A reinforced concrete structure, supported on large mushroom columns permits this free use of space: the unobstructed ceilings that results means no barriers for conveyor belts. The sheer metal and glass curtain wall that wraps the structure employs an innovatory 'sandwich' panelling for thermal insulation.

☐

architect

Gerrit Rietveld

276 Prins Hendrikslaan 50
Utrecht

The abstract geometries of the De Stijl group of avant-garde artists had their greatest built representation in the Schröder house. Rietveld began his association with De Stijl in 1919, only two years after its founding, but he had already been working in their geometric style, most notably with his Red-Blue chair of 1918. But Rietveld carried his work to its best form in the asymmetrical, interlocking, independent planes of the Schröder house. Designed in collaboration with its owner, the house originally faced an expanse of farmland. So the planes of the house, bursting out of normal volumetric confines, expand out into the countryside. Inside the small house, Rietveld has maximised the limited space through a series of interpenetrating cubicles for foyer, kitchen, studio, work and sleeping on the ground floor. On the first floor, in a manner similar to traditional Japanese houses, sliding panels subdivide the sleeping, living, working and dining areas.
☐

Vredenburg Music Centre 1978

architect

Herman Hertzberger

277 Vredenburg
Utrecht

Although it is built out of familiar modern materials: concrete blocks, glass blocks, steel, the Vredenburg Music Centre rebels against the dominant ethos of twentieth-century architecture, functionalism. For Hertzberger does not neatly separate diverse functions; instead, as in a city, there are collisions of purpose and use, a rich mixture of functions. Hertzberger attempts to create the same complexity that results from the natural passage of time in unplanned settlements. So the music centre is far more than a music centre: in addition to a large 1,700-seat auditorium and a 250-seat recital hall, there are shops, restaurants, cafés all jostling for attention. The foyers and corridors become internal piazzas and streets. And as with Centraal Beheer, Apeldoorn ◇ 266, the music centre is an anti-monumental building. Next to the atrocious gigantism of the Hoog Catharijne shopping and office centre, Hertzberger's work is broken down into manageable fragments, composed of his usual vocabulary of details and materials. The mundane materials Hertzberger uses are the one major problem with his architecture, for the very anti-élitist use of industrial materials in a fairly brutal way, which does attract a wide range of users to the centre, also encourages graffiti and litter. But Hertzberger's forms are strong enough to bear such defacing.
□

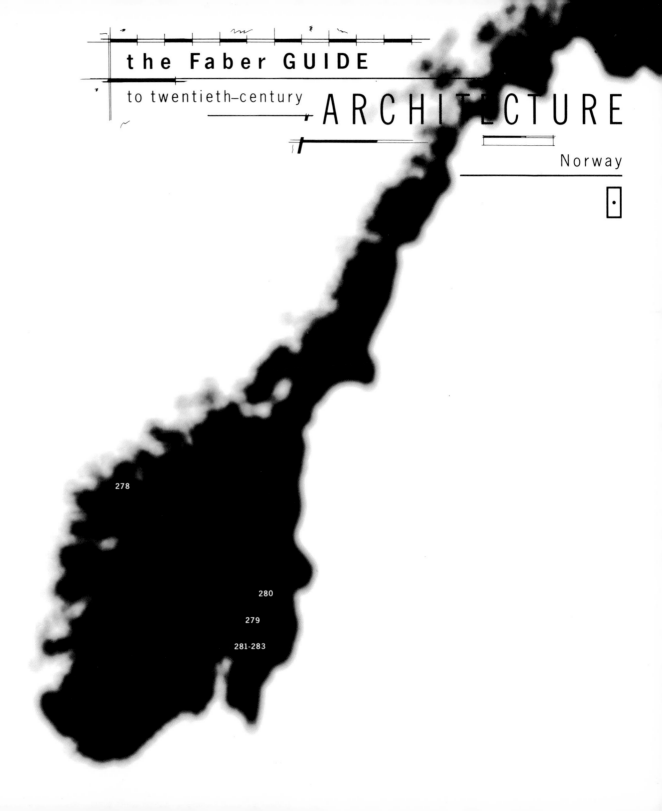

the Faber GUIDE

to twentieth-century ARCHITECTURE

Norway

278

280

279

281-283

Occasionally, natural disaster and architectural history unite to create an outburst of activity. The great Chicago fire of 1870 is probably the best-known example, when the entire city burnt down: as a result, all of the best young architects hurried to Chicago because of the enormous opportunities to build. On a different scale, the town of Aalesund, 240 kilometres south-west of Trondheim on Norway's west coast, is similarly richly endowed with architecture. Although Aalesund was founded in 1848, in 1904 a disastrous fire razed the town to the ground. So the best and brightest of Norway's young architects rushed to rebuild Aalesund. Fortunately for Aalesund, the prevailing style amongst the young bloods of the time was Jugendstil, with its exuberant decoration and unusual shapes. So the centre of Aalesund is crammed with Jugendstil buildings of every description. Of particular note is the old pharmacy in the harbour square with its perfectly preserved interior, but the richness of Aalesund's Jugendstil architecture is best understood by wandering through the streets at random and noting the variations invented for each house, shop, warehouse, etc.

Aal chapel 1929

Gran | **279** | architect **Magnus Poulsson**

Poulsson is widely known for his collaboration with Arnstein Arneberg on the Oslo city hall ◇ 283, but some of his best work is out of the capital. In the Aal chapel, Poulsson achieves a rare blend of monumentalism and the vernacular: the simple lines of the wooden church recall Norway's medieval traditions, but everything here is over-scaled and simplified. The return to ancient building traditions parallels the earlier work of the National Romantics in Scandinavia, but the Aal chapel has none of the rich, craftsmen's decoration which characterises the work of the first decade of the century. □

Hedmark museum 1973

Storhamarlaaven
Hamar | **280** | architect **Sverre Fehn**

The Hedmark museum is built within and on the remains of a medieval bishop's palace. Fehn's aim was to preserve the old stone walls that remain, but also to make the diggings the principal feature of the museum. So Fehn created what he calls a 'suspended' museum: one that rests on and over the archaeology. The main walls are the actual masonry walls of the old palace, but these are augmented with walls of exposed concrete. Concrete is also used for the walkways and ramps that guide visitors through the museum. In contrast, the roof and its supports are made from laminated timber. Fehn's intricate timber details act as counterpoint to the unadorned concrete. □

Government building 1904

Akersgaten 42
Oslo

281

architect **Henrik Bull**

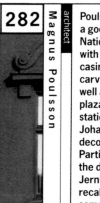

Bull is known for his National Theatre on Stortingsgaten (1899), but the massive government building of 1904 is perhaps more interesting in terms of its antecedents. Bull's work seems to be a misplaced building by the great American architect Henry Hobson Richardson, with its massive rusticated base, floors of roughly hewn stone above and the tell-tale Romanesque arches of the windows. Bull must surely have been familiar with Richardson's work, particularly the Marshall Field Wholesale Store, Chicago (1885-7), for this is one of the most Richardsonian buildings in Europe.
□

DFDS building 1918

Karl Johans Gate 1
Oslo

282

architect **Magnus Poulsson**

Poulsson's DFDS building is a good example of his early National Romantic style, with its picturesque window casings and intricate stone carvings. The building works well as a pivot between the plaza in front of the railway station and the wide Karl Johans Gate because of its decorative tower. Particularly interesting is the doorway on the Jernbane Torvet which recalls the entrance to some medieval town house. The strict symmetry of the composition, however, betrays its modern date.
□

City hall 1931-50

Raadhusplassen
Oslo

283

architect

Arneberg and Poulsson

Although Arneberg and Poulsson won the competition for the city hall in 1920, they were not able to start building until 1931. Although the design changed over these years of waiting, it was clear from the start that they had abandoned the nationalism of their earlier work for a more monumental style. The massive building that resulted acts as a heavy anchor for Oslo, looming over the harbour. The main entrance is opposite the harbour side, through a raised open courtyard flanked by square-columned cloisters. But this pleasant progression is dwarfed by the 60-metre-high office towers. Both the towers and the large block to the south containing the main public rooms are a bit too plain and unadorned for their scale in a city like Oslo.

286-294

284-285

Art gallery 1919-23

Götaplatsen
Gothenburg

architect

Ericson and Bjerke

284 Ericson and Bjerke, as part of the Ares Consortium, directed the Jubilee exhibition of 1923 in Gothenburg, of which the art gallery formed a central part. The unadorned Classical style of the gallery, with the tall rounded arches marching regularly across the entrance, is an extreme of the Scandinavian Classicism of the period. Ericson and Bjerke were also responsible for the design of the Götaplatsen, which borrows its form from Michelangelo's Campidoglio in Rome. The fountain at the centre is Carl Milles' Poseidon.
☐

City theatre 1934

Götaplatsen
Gothenburg

285

architect

Carl Bergsten

Bergsten's theatre lies on the left side of the monumental Götaplatsen, and it is a curious amalgam of Classical and almost whimsical art deco details. The main block of the now ivy-covered building seems fairly plain, with a first-floor gallery of abstracted Ionic columns the main detail of note. Closer examination reveals, however, that the columns have been slipped slightly to the right of centre in their bays, perhaps emphasising their purely decorative role in the structure. The entrance canopy is cantilevered, but additional support is provided by the rather kitsch caryatids (perhaps the caryatids for the entrance to Lubetkin's Highpoint 2, London [1938] were borrowed from Bergsten). The effect of the whole is curious for an architect primarily known for bringing the ideas of the German Werkbund to Sweden.
☐

Engelbrekt church 1909-14

Engelbrekts Kyrkogatan
Stockholm

architect
Lars Israel Wahlman

286 Lars Israel Wahlman was the foremost church architect in Sweden in the first half of the twentieth century, working in a highly personal style that was strongly related to Swedish National Romanticism, the indigenous Arts and Crafts movement. The greatest of Wahlman's works, the Engelbrekt church, stands high on a hill overlooking central Stockholm. Faced in dark-red brick, with decorative pink granite and red sandstone, the church is organised around its tall tower. The tower rises from the top of a series of steps and terraces cut into the hill, using similar materials and details to those found in the church itself. Inside, paraboloid arches of hand-hewn granite reach up to 32 metres above the church floor. Furniture and fittings were also designed by Wahlman, while paintings were done by contemporary Swedish artists.

□

City Hall 1911-23

Hantverkargatan
Stockholm

architect

Ragnar Östberg

287 Östberg's city hall is one
of the best products of
the Scandinavian National
Romantic movement, which sought
to express in architecture the local
and national traditions and visions.
But in its setting and details, the
Stockholm city hall is far more
than an expression of native
traditions: it recalls the Doge's
Palace in Venice, and borrows
references from both Classical
and medieval architecture. While
the various architectural elements
recall the history of Western, and
particularly Swedish, architecture,
the sculptures, carvings, frescoes,
mosaics and tapestries explicitly
relate the history of Stockholm
itself, in much the same manner as
the decorations on a Gothic
cathedral tell theological tales.
The city hall is organised around
two internal courtyards, the open
Civic Court and the covered Blue
Hall. A piano nobile first floor
contains the main ceremonial and
public rooms, the Golden Chamber
and the council chamber.
Throughout there is a carefully
ordered progression from room to
room, an architectural attempt to
heighten the ceremonial aspect of
the building. Thus to pass from the
base of the large bell-tower to the
Golden Chamber, one passes
under the 40-metre-high Arch of
the Hundred to the Oval Room,
which leads to the long gallery
along the waterfront, through the
Round Room to the cubic Three
Crowns Room (expressed on the
exterior by the vaguely Palladian
window with a balcony), then turns
and at last enters the Golden
Chamber. The long hallways
throughout the city hall, the use of
transitional spaces before one
enters the principal rooms, recall
the architecture of medieval
palaces or castles.
□

Högalid church 1911-23

Högalids Park
Stockholm

architect

Ivar Tengbom

288 The conscious transcription of traditional, mainly medieval features, characteristic of the National Romantic style, can clearly be seen in Tengbom's Högalid church. The two towers, which symbolise the Law and the Gospel, are a borrowing from the two towers of St Mary's church, Visby. But much of the church's form is deeply influenced by the work of Tengbom's contemporary Lars Wahlman, and particularly his Engelbrekt's church, designed in 1906 and constructed 1909-14 ◇ 286. The similar site, at the top of a hill overlooking Stockholm, in particular emphasises the stylistic connection between the two works.

One enters through the ornately carved stone of the west portals, and passes through an entrance hall, whose huge beams were decorated by Karl Filip Mansson, who also executed the decorative painting in the church. Although many artists collaborated on the interior, most of the work was Tengbom's own: he designed most of the furnishings as well as some of the objects, such as the silver communion vessels. After the external similarities between Tengbom's and Wahlman's work, however, Tengbom's interior seems stark and bare compared to the rich decoration of the Engelbrekt church.
□

Woodland chapel 1918-20

Skogskyrkogarden
Enskede, Stockholm

architect

Erik Gunnar Asplund

289 When the new southern cemetery was being built in Stockholm, Asplund was given the commission for a small chapel, as cheap as possible, to be built as speedily as possible, to serve until the main chapel was completed. The result is a simple Doric temple, that sits unobtrusively subordinate to the tall, straight pine and fir trees all around. The traditional timber structure is built on a concrete foundation. Walls are externally rendered and internally rough plastered. The roof is covered in layers of pine shingles, while the floors are finished in greyish-brown limestone.

The vestibule to the chapel is supported by twelve timber Doric columns. As one approaches, one notices the sculptor Carl Milles' chased copper and gold angel of death glimmering against the black shingles. Through the open-work iron gate one sees into the light space of the chapel. The room is square, but in contrast to the prevailing straight lines of the exterior and the trees surrounding, the timber columns, grey with painted fluting, are arranged in a circle. A shallow dome above admits light into the chapel. The circular contrast is further accentuated by the floor within the eight columns being sunken two small steps.
□

Odengatan 51-5
Stockholm

architect

Erik Gunnar Asplund

290 Erik Gunnar Asplund's Stockholm city library is a direct descendant of the Barrière de la Villette (1784-9) by the French visionary Claude Nicolas Ledoux. The use of elemental forms, the circle and the square, the cylinder and the cube, marks the start of Asplund's Modern style, in contrast to his earlier Classical and traditional buildings. But the geometric nature of the work shows Asplund's clear debt to the Classical tradition: the library uses the pure forms of Classicism, but strips them of their decorative overlays. Asplund's library was the first in Sweden to have open book-stacks, and the central cylinder was justified on the functional grounds of providing the shortest possible distance between the books and the lending-hall counter. The central lending-hall is top-lit, allowing for a three-tiered circle of books on the circumference. Reading-rooms, light-wells and stairs to other secondary areas are located around this central hall. On the ground floor, directly beneath the lending-hall, are closed stacks for storage.

The library is constructed of brick and concrete, while the roof over the lending-hall is of steel construction with sheet-copper cladding. The external façade, internal walls and ceilings are rendered. The furniture and fittings throughout the library were designed by Asplund with Gustaf Bergström.

□

Concert House 1920-6

Hötorget Stockholm	**291**
architect	
Ivar Tengbom	

Ivar Tengbom's Concert House, with its simple, cubic form, and tall, spindly Corinthian columns, foreshadows the stripped Classicism of the 1930s in Europe and the United States. Tengbom's work was the result of a 1920 competition jointly won by Tengbom and Erik Lallerstedt. The constructional simplicity and relatively low cost of the Tengbom design prevailed in the end. The exterior starkness of the design is slightly offset by the unusual use of a cobalt-blue render, but the main interest lies in the work's interior.
Two auditoria, each with its own cloakrooms and foyer, are packed into the cube. The large auditorium was conceived by Tengbom as a giant room, with a continuous cornice linking the audience area and stage. A trompe-l'œil

painted at the back of the stage (now destroyed) emphasised the continuity of the space. A tall, Corinthian colonnade marches around the auditorium, supporting the galleries and also echoing the external colonnade on Hötorget. In a description of the concert hall upon its opening, Tengbom said the roof above the auditorium 'should have been a glowing southern sky'. Lacking this, he had a canvas 'sun' tent stretched across and lit up at night. Recent renovations have, however, replaced this with a dark ceiling because of lighting requirements.
☐

Swedish Match Company building 1928

Västra Trädgardsgatan 15 Stockholm	**292**	Tengbom's Classical building for the Swedish
architect		
Ivar Tengbom		

Match Company combines ingenious planning with a wide array of idiosyncratic Classical details. The façade, which once overlooked the Kungsträdgarden park, is tripartite: a central bay with a structural Corinthian portico is smoothly rendered, but the two flanking bays are rusticated for their entire height. Hence, the impression from the park was once monumental (there are now no views through), but the large mass is broken up in the oblique views on the narrow street. The central element is further emphasised by the balcony, which serves the directors' rooms. Through the portico, one enters an open semicircular court. The double-height boardroom overlooks this court from the second floor. Two other courts, the garage and the share-registration room, are glazed to allow more light into the enclosed building. Unfortunately, an intermediate floor has recently been added to the double-height share-registration room. Internal corridors are grouped around these two glazed courts so natural light can penetrate.
☐

Chapel of the Holy Cross 1935-40

| Skogskyrkogarden Enskede, Stockholm | **293** |

architect
Erik Gunnar Asplund

With his last work, Asplund's particular blend of Classicism and Modern architecture reached its zenith. The complex of three small chapels for the crematorium of the Woodland cemetery also displays Asplund's skill in integrating buildings and landscape. The crematorium is approached up a long, slow slope, with rolling hills of grass to one side and the low wall of the columbarium to the other. The posts and lintels of the white marble loggia (an extreme of stripped Classicism) progressively reveal themselves, with the large free-standing cross clearly announcing the chapel's presence. The loggia leads to the main chapel. The front wall of the chapel is a metal grille which can be sunk into the floor, allowing the chapel and loggia to become a single linked space to

accommodate large congregations. All the surfaces of the complex are smooth, completely unadorned stone: Asplund achieves his effect through the composition of parts, which is almost Greek in its rigorous Classicism.

☐

Library 1982

| University of Stockholm Frescati, Stockholm | **294** |

architect
Ralph Erskine

In the sixties and seventies, the Frescati campus of the University of Stockholm was laden with banal system-built monoliths, creating an environment without any of the communal, academic aura that should surround universities. In the eighties the university turned to Ralph Erskine for some desperately needed remedial work. Erskine has built three large buildings at Frescati, each of which attempts to stitch together the campus and to provide community spaces that were sorely lacking. The most important of these Erskine buildings is the 24,000 m² library, which adjoins the seventies Södra Huset (which houses the faculties of law, social sciences and humanities). A giant railway-shed-like roof encloses the entrance, which becomes an internal plaza, usable in the harsh Stockholm winters. White, round concrete columns line this plaza, supporting the arching timber beams with branch-like steel struts. The library attached to the shed is a large square, with its south-east corner eroded away to encircle four ancient oak trees that are remnants of the royal deer park that used to be on the site. Throughout the library, Erskine mixes a variety of materials in his eclectic style: concrete panels clad the ground floor, window frames are timber, steel panels make a further division, and the roof is clad in hand-beaten stainless steel.

☐

Select Bibliography

Banham, Reyner	**The architecture of the well-tempered environment**	London, The Architectural Press, 1969
Banham, Reyner	**Theory and design in the first machine age**	London, The Architectural Press, 1960
Benevolo, Leonardo	**History of modern architecture,** two volumes	London, Routledge & Kegan Paul, 1971
Conrads, Ulrich, editor	**Programmes and manifestos on twentieth-century architecture**	London, Lund Humphries, 1970
Frampton, Kenneth	**Modern architecture: a critical history**	London, Thames & Hudson, 1980
Hitchcock, Henry-Russell	**Architecture: nineteenth and twentieth centuries**	Harmondsworth, Penguin Books, 1977
Jencks, Charles	**Modern movements in architecture**	Harmondsworth, Penguin Books, 1973
Le Corbusier	**Towards a new architecture**	London, The Architectural Press, 1946
Pehnt, Wolfgang	**Expressionist architecture**	London, Thames & Hudson, 1973
Pevsner, Nikolaus	**Pioneers of modern design: from William Morris to Walter Gropius**	Harmondsworth, Penguin Books, 1975
Placzek, Adolf, editor	**Macmillan encyclopedia of architects,** four volumes	West Drayton, Collier Macmillan, 1982
Wingler, Hans Maria	**The Bauhaus: Weimar, Dessau, Berlin, Chicago**	Cambridge, MIT Press, 1969

1898–1976
■ Alvar Aalto

1923-4
Railway employees' housing
Jyväskylä Finland

1925
Civil guard house
Seinäjoki Finland

1926
Villa Väinölä
Alajärvi Finland

1927
Municipal hospital
Alajärvi Finland

1927-9
Civil guard house
Jyväskylä Finland

1927-9
Parish church
Muurame Finland

1927-9
South-western Agricultural
Co-operative
Turku Finland

1928-9
Standard apartment for Tapani
Turku Finland

1928-30
Turun Sanomat offices
Turku Finland

1933-5
Municipal library
Viipuri Finland
(now Viborg, USSR)

1938-40
Terraced housing
Kauttua Finland

1946-9
Baker dormitories
Cambridge Massachusetts USA

1953-5
Own house
Muuratsalo Finland

1953-5
Rautatalo office building
Helsinki Finland

1956-9
Maison Louis Carré
Bazoches sur Guyonne France

1958-62
Cultural centre
Wolfsburg West Germany

1959-62
Central Finnish museum
Jyväskylä Finland

1959-62
Enso-Gutzeit offices
Helsinki Finland

1963-8
Library
Rovaniemi Finland

1965-70
Library, Mount Angel Benedictine College
Mount Angel Oregon USA

1969-73
Art museum
Aalborg Denmark

1972-8
Parish centre
Riola Italy

1972-8
Theatre
Rovaniemi Finland

1885–1940
■ Erik Gunnar Asplund

1912-18
Secondary school
Karlshamn Sweden

1913
Villa Selander
Örnsköldsvik Sweden

1914
Villa Ruth
Kuusankoski Finland

1917-18
Villa Snellman
Djursholm Sweden

1917-21
Lister county courthouse
Sölvesborg Sweden

1922-3
Skandia Cinema
Stockholm Sweden

1931
Swedish Society of Arts and Crafts
Stockholm Sweden

1933-7
State bacteriological laboratory
Stockholm Sweden

1934-7
Law courts annexe
Göteborg Sweden

1936-40
Own villa
Stennäs Sweden

1868–1940
■ Peter Behrens

1905-6
Obenauer house
Saarbrücken West Germany

1905-7
Crematorium
Hagen West Germany

1908-10
Catholic lodging house
Neuss West Germany

1909-10
AEG high tension factory
West Berlin

1910-12
Goedecke house
Hagen West Germany

1910-13
AEG small motors factory
West Berlin

1910-15, 1918-19
AEG factories and workers' housing
Hennigsdorf West Germany

1911-12
AEG large machine factory
West Berlin

1911-12
AEG electric railway
equipment factory
West Berlin

1911-12
AEG Rowing Club Elektra
West Berlin

1911-12
German embassy
Leningrad USSR

1911-20
Continental Rubber Company offices
Hanover West Germany

1914
Frank and Lehmann building
Cologne West Germany

1920-1
Deutsche Werft housing
Altona West Germany

1920-4
I.G. Farben offices
Frankfurt-Hoechst West Germany

1921-5
Gutehoffnungshütte offices and warehouse
Oberhausen West Germany

1923-6
Bassett-Lowke house
Northampton England

1924-5
St Peter's monastery
Salzburg Austria

1924-9
Low-income housing
Vienna Austria

1926-7
Terrace house apartments
Stuttgart West Germany

1929-30
Kurt Lewin house
West Berlin

1929-31
Alexanderplatz offices
East Berlin

1930
Bolivarallee apartments
West Berlin

1931-2
Clara Ganz villa
Kronberg im Taunus West Germany

1932-4
State tobacco factory
Linz Austria

1856–1934
■ Hendrik Petrus Berlage

1884-6
Focke and Meltzer store
Amsterdam Netherlands

1891-2
E.D. Pijzel house
Amsterdam Netherlands

1894
G. Heymans house
Groningen Netherlands

1894-5
De Nederlanden van 1845 Insurance
Company offices
Amsterdam Netherlands

1895-6
De Nederlanden van 1845 Insurance
Company offices
The Hague Netherlands

1898
Carel Henny house
The Hague Netherlands

1899-1901
Diamond Workers' Union
Amsterdam Netherlands

1902
De Algemeene
Leipzig East Germany

1906
Voorwaarts Workers' Cooperative
Rotterdam Netherlands

1910-13
Tolstraat housing
Amsterdam Netherlands

1911-13
Transvaalbuurt housing
Amsterdam Netherlands

1912-15
Javaplein housing
Amsterdam Netherlands

1913
Own house
The Hague Netherlands

1914
Meddens and Son
The Hague Netherlands

1915-19
Sint Hubertus hunting lodge
Otterlo Netherlands

1924-7
De Nederlanden van 1845 Insurance
Company offices
Amsterdam Netherlands

1925-32
Amsterdamse Bank
Amsterdam Netherlands

1927-35
Gemeentemuseum
The Hague Netherlands

1929
Town hall
Usquert Netherlands

1883–1969
■ Walter Gropius

1925-6
Bauhaus
Dessau East Germany

1926-7
Toerten housing
Dessau East Germany

1931
Copper houses
Finow East Germany

1936
Levy house (with Maxwell Fry)
London England

1937
Own house (with Marcel Breuer)
Lincoln Massachusetts USA

1939
Frank house
Pittsburgh Pennsylvania USA

1941
Housing (with Breuer)
New Kensington Pennsylvania USA

1948
Junior High School
(with The Architects Collaborative)
Attleboro Massachusetts USA

1949-50
Harvard University graduate centre
(with TAC)
Cambridge Massachusetts USA

1955
Interbau housing (with TAC)
West Berlin

1956
United States embassy (with TAC)
Athens Greece

1957
Pan-Am Building (with Pietro Belluschi)
New York City New York USA

1957
University (with TAC)
Baghdad Iraq

1958
Temple Oheb Shalom (with TAC)
Baltimore Maryland USA

1963
Rosenthal ceramics factory (with TAC)
Selb West Germany

1967
Tower East office building
Cleveland Ohio USA

1968
Huntington Gallery (with TAC)
Huntington West Virginia USA

1968
J.F.K. federal office building
Boston Massachusetts USA

1867–1942
■ Hector Guimard

1893
Jassède house
Paris France

1893
Roszel house
Paris France

1895
Ecole du Sacré-Coeur
Paris France

1902-5
Nozal house
Paris France

1910-11
Mezzara house
Paris France

1911-13
Synagogue rue Pavée
Paris France

1861–1947
■ Victor Horta

1889-1905
Lambeaux sculpture pavilion
Brussels Belgium

1890
Mattyn house
Brussels Belgium

1892-3
Tassel house
Brussels Belgium

1894
Frison house
Brussels Belgium

1894-1903
Winssinger house
Brussels Belgium

1895-1908
Van Eetvelde houses
Brussels Belgium

1899
Aubecq house
Brussels Belgium

1903-28
Tournai museum
Brussels Belgium

1906-26
Brugmann hospital
Brussels Belgium

1911-37
Central railway station
(completed after 1945 by
Maxim Brunfaut)
Brussels Belgium

1920-8
Palais des Beaux-Arts
Brussels Belgium

1888–1965
■ Le Corbusier

1905-6
Villa Fallet
La Chaux-de-Fonds Switzerland

1907-8
Villa Jaquemet
La Chaux-de-Fonds Switzerland

1911-12
Villa Jeanneret
La Chaux-de-Fonds Switzerland

1912-13
Villa Favre-Jacot
Le Locle Switzerland

1916
Cinema La Scala
La Chaux-de-Fonds Switzerland

1916-17
Villa Schwob
La Chaux-de-Fonds Switzerland

1922
Villa Besnus
Vaucresson France

1923-4
Villa Le Lac
Vevey Switzerland

1925
Cité Fruges housing
Pessac France

1928
Villa Baizeau
Carthage Tunisia

1928-34
Centrosoyous
Moscow USSR

1930-2
Immeuble Clarté housing
Geneva Switzerland

1935
Own villa
Les Mathes France

1936-45
Ministry of National Education and
Public Health Building
Rio de Janeiro Brazil

1946
Claude et Duval factory
Sainte-Dié France

1948
Villa Currutchet
La Plata Argentina

1951-6
High court
Chandigarh India

1951-7
Museum
Ahmedabad India

1952-3
Unité d'habitation
Rézé-les-Nantes France

1952-4
Mill Owners Association
Ahmedabad India

1952-5
Villa Sarabhai
Ahmedabad India

1952-6
Secretariat
Chandigarh India

1953-63
Palace of the Assembly
Chandigarh India

1956
Villa Shodan
Ahmedabad India

1956-9
Museum of Western Art
Tokyo Japan

1960-3
Carpenter Center for the Visual Arts
Harvard University
Cambridge Massachusetts USA

1962-
Church
Firminy France (unfinished)

1963-5
Nautical club
Chandigarh India

1963-7
Maison de l'Homme
Zurich Switzerland

1964-8
Museum and art gallery
Chandigarh India

1870–1933
■ Adolf Loos

1899
Museum café
Vienna Austria

1907
Kaerntner bar
Vienna Austria

1910
Steiner house
Vienna Austria

1910-11
Goldman & Salatsch store
Vienna Austria

1912
Scheu house
Vienna Austria

1928
Moller house
Vienna Austria

1930
Mueller house
Prague Czechoslovakia

1901–
■ Berthold Lubetkin

1927-31
Housing (with Jean Ginsberg)
Paris France

1932-3
Gorilla house (with Tecton),
London Zoo
London England

1934-5
Whipsnade Zoo buildings (with Tecton)
Whipsnade England

1936-7
Dudley Zoo buildings (with Tecton)
Dudley England

1937-51
Priory Green housing (with Tecton)
London England

1938-46
Spa Green housing (with Tecton)
London England

1947-55
Hallfield housing (with Tecton)
London England

1869–1944
■ Edwin Lutyens

1891
Munstead Place
Munstead England

1892
Red House
Effingham England

1896-7
Munstead Wood
Munstead England

1897-9
Hazelhatch
Burrows Cross England

1897-9
Orchards
Munstead England

1898
Le Bois des Moutiers
Varengeville-sur-Mer France

1899-1901
Overstrand Hall
Cromer England

1899-1901
Tigbourne Court
Witley England

1900-1
Grey Walls
Gullane Scotland

1901
Homewood
Knebworth England

1901-4
Marshcourt
Stockbridge England

1902
Little Thakeham
Thakeham England

1903-4
Lindisfarne Castle (restoration)
Holy Island England

1904
Country Life building
London England

1905-12
Lambay Castle
Ireland

1906
Folly Farm
Sulhampstead England

1907
Fisher's Hill Cottage
Woking England

1909
Great Maytham
Rolvenden England

1910
Great Dixter
Northiam England

1911
The Salutation
Sandwich England

1912-31
Viceroy's House complex
(now Rashtrapati Bhavan)
New Delhi India

1914
Mausoleum,
Golder's Green crematorium
London England

1919
Count de Cimera house
Madrid Spain

1920-4
Britannic House
London England

1921-3
Palace for the Gaekwar of Baroda
New Delhi India

1921-5
Midland Bank, Piccadilly
London England

1922-6
Gledstone Hall
Gledstone England

1926
Palace for the Nizam of Hyderabad
New Delhi India

1927-8
British embassy
Washington Washington DC USA

1928-32
Magdalene College (various buildings)
Cambridge England

1934
Cedar House
Chobham England

1935
Reuters and Press Association
London England

1935-42
Campion Hall
Oxford England

1938
Middleton Park (with Robert Lutyens)
Middleton England

1868–1928
■ Charles Rennie Mackintosh

1890
Redclyffe
Springburn Scotland

1893
Glasgow Herald building tower
(with John Keppie)
Glasgow Scotland

1894-6
Queen Margaret's medical college
(with Keppie)
Glasgow Scotland

1895
Martyr's public school (with Keppie)
Glasgow Scotland

1897-9
Queen's Cross Church of Scotland
Glasgow Scotland

1898
Ruchill Street church halls
Glasgow Scotland

1899-1901
Windy Hill
Kilmacolm Scotland

1901
Daily Record offices
Glasgow Scotland

1903-10
Hous'hill
Nitshill Scotland

1906
Mosside
Kilmacolm Scotland

1906
Own house
(now in Hunterian Art Gallery)
Glasgow Scotland

1906
Auchinibert (now Cloak)
Killearn Scotland

1916-20
Bassett-Lowke house (interiors)
Northampton England

1887–1953
■ Eric Mendelsohn

1919-24
Einstein Tower
Potsdam East Germany

1921-3
Herman and Company hat factory
Luckenwalde East Germany

1928-9
Schocken department store
Karl-Marx-Stadt East Germany

1929
Own house
West Berlin

1934-6
Weizmann house
Rehovot Israel

1936
Schocken library
Jerusalem Israel

1937-8
Government hospital
Haifa Israel

1937-9
Hadassah University medical centre
Jerusalem Israel

1939
Agricultural Institute
Rehovot Israel

1946-50
B'nai Amoona temple and
community centre
St Louis Missouri USA

1946-50
Maimonides health center
San Francisco California USA

1948-52
Emanu-El temple and community centre
Grand Rapids Michigan USA

1950-1
Russell house
San Francisco California USA

1950-4
Mount Zion temple and community centre
St Paul Minnesota USA

1888–1969
■ Ludwig Mies van der Rohe

1907
Riehl house
Neubabelsberg East Germany

1911
Perls house
West Berlin

1919-21
Kempner house
West Berlin

1928
Lange house
Krefeld West Germany

1928-30
Tugendhat house
Brno Czechoslovakia

1939-56
Illinois Institute of Technology
Chicago Illinois USA

1945-50
Farnsworth house
Plano Illinois USA

1948-51
860 and 880
Lake Shore Drive apartments
Chicago Illinois USA

1954-8
Cullinan Hall, Museum of Fine Arts
Houston Texas USA

1954-8
Seagram Building
New York City New York USA

1955-6
Lafayette Park housing
Detroit Michigan USA

1957-61
Bacardi offices
Mexico City Mexico

1959-73
Chicago Federal Center
Chicago Illinois USA

1960-3
American Federal Savings and
Loan Association
Des Moines Iowa USA

1963-9
Toronto Dominion Centre
Toronto Ontario Canada

1890–1963
■ J. J. P. Oud

1906
Alida Hartog-Oud house
Purmerend Netherlands

1911
Vooruit co-operative housing
Purmerend Netherlands

1912
Schinkel cinema
Purmerend Netherlands

1914
Van Bakel house
Heemstede Netherlands

1914-16
Leiderdorp housing (with W. M. Dudok)
Leiderdorp Netherlands

1915
Van Essen-Vincker house
Blaricum Netherlands

1917-19
De Vonk vacation retreat
(with Theo van Doesburg)
Noordwijkerhout Netherlands

1918-20
Spangen housing
Rotterdam Netherlands

1920
Tusschendijken housing
Rotterdam Netherlands

1922-3
Oud-Mathensee housing
Rotterdam Netherlands

1925-9
Kiefhoek housing
Rotterdam Netherlands

1928-9
Kiefhoek church
Rotterdam Netherlands

1938-42
Shell offices
The Hague Netherlands

1943
Central savings bank
Rotterdam Netherlands

1947-50
Esveha offices
Rotterdam Netherlands

1950-6
Lyceum
The Hague Netherlands

1952-60
Bio convalescent resort for children
Arnhem Netherlands

1954-61
Utrecht Life Insurance Company
Rotterdam Netherlands

1957-63
Convention centre
The Hague Netherlands

1873–1950
■ Eliel Saarinen

1897
Tallberg apartments
Helsinki Finland

1901
Olofsborg apartments
(with Gesellius and Lindgren)
Helsinki Finland

1902-3
Suur-Merijoki
(with Gesellius and Lindgren)
Viborg USSR

1904-13
Railway station
Viborg USSR

1909-13
Town hall
Joensun Finland

1916-18
Villa Keirkner
Helsinki Finland

1920
Kästyöläisankki building
Helsinki Finland

1924-30
Cranbrook school for boys
Bloomfield Hills Michigan USA

1928-9
Own house
Bloomfield Hills Michigan USA

1929-30
Hudnut building
(with Ely Jacques Kahn)
New York City New York USA

1929-30
Kingswood school for girls
Bloomfield Hills Michigan USA

1931-3
Cranbrook Institute of Science
Bloomfield Hills Michigan USA

1938-40
Kleinhans music hall
Buffalo New York USA

1939-40
Crow Island school (with Eero Saarinen)
Winnetka Illinois USA

1939-42
Tabernacle Church of Christ
(with Eero Saarinen)
Columbus Indiana USA

1940-3
Cranbrook museum and library
Bloomfield Hills Michigan USA

1893–1972
■ Hans Scharoun

1917
Community hall
Kattenau Poland

1920
Two houses
Insterburg
(now Chernyakhovsk, USSR)

1922
Single-family houses
Insterburg
(now Chernyakhovsk, USSR)

1923-4
Housing
Insterburg
(now Chernyakhovsk, USSR)

1924-5
Public buildings
Bad Mergentheim Spa West Germany

1933
Schminke house
Löbau East Germany

1937-8
Noack house
Potsdam East Germany

1940
Kaiserstrasse housing
Bremerhaven West Germany

1949
Institute of Building,
German Academy of Sciences
West Berlin

1954-9
Romeo and Juliet housing,
Zuffenhausen
Stuttgart West Germany

1956-62
Geschwister school
Lünen West Germany

1961-8
School
Marl West Germany

1963-71
German embassy
Brasilia Brazil

1965-73
City theatre
Wolfsburg West Germany

1966
Architecture building,
Technical University of Berlin
West Berlin

1966
St John chapel
Bochum West Germany

1967-78
State Library
West Berlin

1970
Rabenberg church
Wolfsburg West Germany

1970
German maritime museum
Bremerhaven West Germany

1870–1956
■ Lars Eliel Sonck

1895
Lasses Villa, Bartsgarda
Finström Finland

1896
Villa Skogshyddan, Mariehamn
Åland Islands Finland

1904
Villa Ainola
Järvenpää Finland

1905
Eira hospital
Helsinki Finland

1908
Mortgage society building
Helsinki Finland

1909-12
Kallio church
Helsinki Finland

1915
Kulosaari fire station
Helsinki Finland

1927
Mariehamn church
Åland Islands Finland

1935
Mikael Agricola church
(with Arvo Muroma)
Helsinki Finland

1939
Town hall, Mariehamn
Åland Islands Finland

1926–
■ James Stirling

1956
House (with James Gowan)
Isle of Wight England

1957
Ham Common low-rise flats
(with Gowan)
London England

1958-61
Dining-hall, Brunswick Park
primary school
(with Gowan)
London England

1960-4
Home for the elderly (with Gowan)
Blackheath
London England

1964
Andrew Melville Hall,
University of St Andrews
Scotland

1965
Dorman Long headquarters
Middlesbrough England

1966
Florey Building, Queen's College
Oxford England

Index